Secrets Best Untol(

Book Three of the

Copyright © Augu

This is a work of fiction. Names, characters, places, and incidents are the product of the author's imagination. Any resemblance to actual persons, living or dead, events or locations is entirely coincidental.

Cover Art provided by Jay Aheer of Simply Defined Art

Editing provided by Pam Ebeler of Undivided Editing

All rights reserved. This book is licensed to the original publisher only. No part of this book may be reproduced, scanned or distributed.

This book contains mature content and is only intended for adult readers over the age of 18

Also from this Author

Tales from Edovia Series

Something from Nothing

Buried Truths

Secrets Best Untold

Coming October 2016

Trusting Tanner

(This title will be published under Encompass Ink)

Acknowledgments

It takes a village to write a book. Well, maybe not a village but I couldn't have made this journey alone. As always this book couldn't have been made possible without the help of my fabulous editor Pam Ebeler from Undivided Editing. I owe this woman so much, but most pressing; a box of tissues and a bottle of wine. Thanks you lady with all my heart.

Also, I have to give a shout out to the amazing lady who is Jay Aheer from Simply Defined Art for designing my cover art once again. Without her patience in trying to understand my crazy mind, this gorgeousness may not have happened. You are the best, Jay.

Lastly, thank you to the crazy man who puts up with me daily and has been my pillar since day one. I love you Jamie.

Dedication

This series conclusion is for all those people who have made it this far with my boys. Thank you for taking this journey.

Secrets Best Untold

Jay:

Love has no boundaries ♡

Take good care of my sweet boys ♡

♡ Ricky James xoxo

<u>Prologue</u>

You already know my happy ending. It wasn't a "Once upon a time", fairy tale type story either. It had its ups and downs as any story does. There were bumps in our road and thorns in our sides, but we won our freedom in the end. Not only the freedom of our lives and to take our next breath, but the freedom to love. I won my Alistair. It was a happy ending as I never imagined I would find in this lifetime. I had a gorgeous man by my side who loved me with all his heart and soul; the same love I gave to him in return.

I'm a simple man and this alone brought me more happiness and joy than I had ever known. But my journey to get there wasn't easy or what you may expect.

Growing up, I travelled down a road no child should ever have to travel and kept secrets no child should ever have to keep. Through my quest to find a better, happier life, I had to create my new identity; Brandon Leeson. This is the only man anyone knows me as anymore. His purpose was for new beginnings. He put an end to the horrors of my past...or was supposed to.

I thought, with his creation, I could leave the demons from my childhood behind; buried deep...with Jeremy. I thought that desolate place from before was nothing more than a dark secret that I could keep hidden away until the end of time, locked up in a clouded over part of my brain I would never access again; especially after finding said "happy ending".

It turns out life can be cruel; doors don't stay locked forever and walls crumble. Secrets get whispered in the wind and somehow, somewhere, somebody hears them.

Sometimes, you have to venture back through that hellish place for a little while and hope it doesn't consume you in the end. Hope and pray that you can fight your way out of the twisted wreckage that has once again become your life without losing yourself in the process.

Hope for strength to survive.

Chapter One

Present Day – Early Spring

Alistair

It's all my fault. If I had stood my ground and not let him go, he would be fine right now. Instead, I may have lost him for good.

The high pitched squeak of wood rubbing on wood rings out across the silent room and alerts me that I have company. Keeping my eyes fixed on the still body of my sleeping lover, I don't bother looking to see who is entering. It doesn't matter. My bed chambers have become everything from meeting room, to surgery, to chapel as of late, and no one bothers to knock anymore.

Since returning to the city, everything has a dream like quality about it, like it isn't quite real; fuzzy at the edges and nondescript. I feel as though I'm wandering through a haze of bustling bodies and muffled noises trying to reach a destination, but I can't get any closer to where I want to be no matter how hard I try. I pray I will wake up at any moment and that everything will be as it once was. Only, this is no dream. This is real.

"You should get some rest." The voice behind me is familiar.

A large hand rests on my shoulder and gives it a squeeze. The touch drains the last of my strength and sets my chin to quiver and my vision to blur. Endless nights without sleep and no answers cause all my efforts at holding myself together to fail with that simple gesture.

Eric Corban squats down beside the chair I have pulled up to the bed and takes my hand in both of his. "Son, you will be no good to him if you don't take care of yourself."

"I can't leave him." My voice cracks as I fight back the tears threatening to fall.

"I'm not asking you to, but close your eyes and try to get some rest."

"What if he doesn't come back to me?" My heart pinches at the reality of my own words.

What if he doesn't want me anymore?

"He will. He loves you. He'll find his way back."

"It's all my fault, Eric."

"You can't blame yourself. Brandon chose to go. Everyone thought it was the right decision-"

"I didn't." I say firmly. "I should have stopped him. I shouldn't have allowed it."

"Alistair, look at me."

Eric's hand is under my chin pulling it around to face him. Fighting against him, I firm my jaw and do what I can to remove any indications of weakness from my face. I hate this crushing feeling of despair that is clinging to me and has been clinging to me all winter. But I can't shake it and I don't want Eric to see the wreck of a man I've become. With barely any fight in me left, his determination is stronger than my will and in the end I meet his strong dark eyes.

Eric is the closest thing I've ever had to a father. I never knew my real father, the late King, Chrystiaan Ellesmere. On his death bed he legitimized my birth with the courts - his only son; his bastard son - and left me everything.

When I was brought back to Ludairium eight years ago to take my place as King of Edovia, Eric took me under his wing and taught me everything I needed to know. Not only did he guide me down the right path and show me the ways of a King, but he embraced me as a son and has stood by my side through some of the hardest moments I have ever had to endure.

The wrinkles on Eric's forehead are more prominent than usual as he searches my face with deep concern. His silver streaked, black hair is a tousled mess and I wonder if he was pulled from his bed to come deal with me. Concern for the health and wellbeing of the King and his lover is running as rampant around the city and castle as the rumors are of how we wound up like this.

"Are you listening?" He asks.

I nod my head and tighten my muscles to try and control the shivers that keep sending my body to quake. They just won't stop.

"This is not your fault. Brandon *is* alive. He *will* come back to you, but you need to rest because when he does, he'll need you. All of you, not a crumpled man who is so sleep deprived he can't function. Do you understand me?"

I nod again. I don't trust my voice.

"Do you want something to help you rest? I can send for Chase."

"No. I'm fine."

His eyes linger on me a while longer. He's probably considering if he should defy me and send for the doctor regardless. It's pointless. I'll only refuse anything Chase offers as I have done since we returned. I need to stay alert for Brandon. *What if he needs me?* Eric knows me too well and instead nods his head with a heavy sigh.

Giving my hand a final squeeze, Eric rises and heads to the door. The eerie squeak echoes through the room again, followed by a muffling click and I'm once again blanketed in silence. The only sound is that of Brandon's deep, labored breathing coming from our bed where he has been curled up for the last few days.

In the early winter, after much planning and organizing, a group of twenty-five of my best soldiers marched north to the border of Edovia. The intent was for them to meet up with an escort of

Outsiders who would take them deep into the enemy territory for a rendezvous with their leader. The purpose of the expedition was to negotiate a truce and prevent a pending war that could have seen my lands easily destroyed. When I say easily, I mean that without a truce, we truly stood no chance of survival. This imminent war had been threatening our lands for far too long.

The Outsiders made a few demands surrounding our peace talks and one of those demands was that I would escort my men and personally hand them over at the border. Maybe we should have listened. I could have done it. I would have, but not a single councilmen agreed that this was wise. Therefore, an alternative plan was contrived. One that did not get my vote.

Brandon was sent in *my* place, meant to impersonate me for the exchange only because it was felt sending me was too risky a move. The Outsiders should have been none the wiser.

To say the mission was a success is only part truth. Terms *were* agreed upon and a truce *was* made, but the one person I love more than life itself came back to me a broken man. He wasn't even supposed to have crossed the border. He was supposed to have strictly been present for the exchange beforehand and nothing more.

It took a single man near on a fortnight of hard, steady riding to bring news to Ludairium of Brandon's crossing. That moment sent my world spiraling out of control and I have yet to stop the spinning. I have only managed to piece together bits of information on what happened. My guesses are the substance of nightmares and I try not to allow my brain to venture into such frightening territory, but sleep deprivation has given me less control over my senses and my blasted mind wanders on its own free will without my consent.

I rub my tired, stinging eyes and stand from the chair where I have been sitting all day. Gripping the edge of the bed, I shake the cramps out of my legs and then stretch.

Apart from a quick shave and wipe down in a lukewarm basin of water a few nights ago, I've hardly taken the time to clean up from my impromptu journey north to bring Brandon home. I feel like half a man at this point, but can't bring myself to rectify the problem. My own well-being is the furthest thing from my concern. My only concern is for Brandon.

Not bothering to undress, knowing the parade of people that can come and go from my rooms on a whim, I climb up on the bed beside Brandon, fully clothed. He is curled up on his side facing away from me, knees tucked up to his chest, arms hugging a piled up mountain of blankets beside him. His grip is so tight it looks as though the blanket is his only anchor to reality and without it he would fall away into nothingness.

Careful not to disturb him, I lay down and edge myself closer. Thinking back on previous nights, my stomach roils with nerves and my chest aches. Fear of rejection wants to hold me back, but a longing to touch Brandon and be close to him always makes me try again, hoping for a different result.

I reach out a shaky hand, trace it gently down over his arm as I snuggle in closer, bringing my body to fit perfectly along his back, pressing into him and burying my face in the crook of his neck. His familiar scent hits my nose and sends my stomach to flip flop around. Maker, how I miss this man.

Ordinarily, this would have been one of our preferred ways of sleeping, second maybe only to Brandon on his back, with my head rested on his shoulder. The loss of such a simple thing sends a pang of sadness to tug at my heart.

As anticipated, the brief moment of joy at having him in my arms again is shattered when the once sleeping body beside me wakes, stiffens at my embrace, and pulls away as though my touches are fire searing into his skin. I don't fight him. I release my hold and stay perfectly still in the center of the bed, holding my breath. Brandon has moved as far over as the bed will allow and is now hovering precariously on the edge. I don't fear he will fall, because he is no longer asleep. His breathing has changed. It is erratic now and if he were facing me I would bet his eyes are wide open and swimming with terror. I know because this isn't the first time.

Moving away from him, inching to the opposite side of the bed, I slide off and return to the chair. Just like last night and every night since his return to Edovia, the man cowers from my touch, shrinking away with a fear I cannot understand. The ache in my chest feels so real that I'm sure my heart is quite literally breaking in half as I sit there in the dark watching him.

The faint glow from the hearth illuminates enough of the room so that I can make out the rise and fall of the blankets covering Brandon. His breathing has quickened and I can see he is on high alert, no doubt thinking I might make another attempt to touch him. I don't.

The feelings of helplessness consume me again. The idea that my touch, the same touch that not that long ago brought pleasure, happiness, and joy, that now brings only dread, prickles tears back to my eyes. I blink them away, trying to force myself to calm, but they fall regardless. I will never stop trying, no matter how many times he pushes me away, I will never stop. I will never give up on him. Despite the thousand and one other responsibilities in my life, Brandon is my only concern.

I don't know for how long I sit watching the rhythm of his breathing, but it finally relaxes to a steadier pace and the tension slowly fades from his body. He is still not asleep, but his fear is subsiding.

"I'm sorry," I whisper into the darkness, "I didn't mean to upset you. I only... I just wanted... I love you, Brandon. I'm sorry." The tight lump in my throat won't go down no matter how many times I swallow.

I don't expect a response so I'm not surprised when I don't get one. I've tried endlessly to coax Brandon to speak to me. I've asked him what happened. I've begged him, I've gotten angry with him, I've demanded. I've cried, I've yelled. Nothing works. He won't meet my eyes and he won't say anything. Any time I try to touch him, he pulls away, never in disgust, but in fear. Fear of what, I have no idea.

Tonight, in the dark quiet of my bed chambers, all I can do is watch while the love of my life lays lost in some kind of waking nightmare inside his head. The result of a supposed "successful" trip across the border. Somehow, this man alone managed to negotiate our way to freedom, but at what cost? What the hell happened to him over there?

Chapter Two

Previous Winter

Alistair

"The moment word arrives; our men will march. I have everyone standing by at the ready. I anticipate it to take no more than the turn of a moon to-"

A sharp knock on the wooden doors to the council chambers halts me mid-sentence, the councilmen and I all turn to see who could possibly be interrupting our meeting.

Without waiting for permission to enter one of my guards, dressed in full leather armor with a sword swinging off his hip, steps through; a look of concern darkening his features.

"Excuse me, gentlemen. I have Darion Waters seeking immediate audience, he says it's an emergency."

"Darion?" The name rolls off my tongue and around my brain. Why does this sound wrong to my ears? Darion? Darion? Wait. Darion is supposed to be up north with the negotiating party. Why is he here? The hairs on my arms rise as I nod my head to the guard, giving permission for him to allow Darion to enter.

The guard opens the door further and Darion Waters comes through looking worse for wear and more distraught than the guard. His hair is a matted, brown mess and he has sweat stains under the arms of his shirt and dirt smeared across his face. He is dressed in full riding gear minus his coat, which he has slung over his arm. There is fresh mud splattered halfway up his boots and his chest heaves with the effort to calm his labored breathing. He looks like a man that has just rode full tilt across the bloody realm in a really big hurry.

The man does a quick scan around the table and when his eyes find me, everyone else is forgotten. He approaches me and bobs his head in subtle greeting. The man knows better than to bow, a gesture anyone who knows me understands only lends to aggravate me. My heart hammers against my ribs as I see the white fear behind Darion's flush cheeks.

"We have a problem." He says.

My mouth goes dry and my tongue feels thick in my mouth. When I speak, my words are hoarse and raspy.

"Brandon?"

I search his eyes while a vice tightens around my heart.

Darion nods. "They weren't fooled. They knew he wasn't you. He," Darion glances to the other men of the council, "he agreed to cross. Alone. H-he went…w-we couldn't stop him."

The man shakes his head, his words stuttering and breaking as he cowers back a step from me. I can feel the heat rising to my face.

"Went? Went where?" I can hear his jumbled words but my brain is having trouble catching up.

"He went to negotiate. Alone." Darion says, meeting my eyes again. "A-a-after they knew it wasn't you…they-th-they changed the rules…h-he agreed to go alone…and… unarmed."

A fire burns in my gut and a flash of pure rage sends me flying at Darion. I grab his shirt front in both my hands and slam him into the wall at his back so hard the man grunts out a wheezing breath. His eyes go wide at my outburst and he can do nothing more than blink at me.

"You let him go alone?" My voice thunders and echoes through the room leaving it in eerie silence.

"He ordered us to stand down…He…They were outraged at the deceit-"

"When? When did he cross?"

"I-I waited five days…They said three…we-we didn't know…I rode back practically non-stop…umm…m-might…might be a fortnight now…I came as fast as I could."

Darion is shaking under the balled up fists I hold around his shirt, but no more than me. My knees wobble as I try to make sense of what he is telling me. He's rambling and I don't understand what he's saying and yet I can't seem to find the right questions to get the right answers.

Brandon crossed the border. Alone. Unarmed. This much I know.

"Alistair. Let him go."

I didn't notice Eric approach or that he has wrapped his hands around mine and is peeling my fingers from Darion's shirt. All I can see is the stunned man's face before me, pupils dilated so far there is no more indication of what color his eyes might be.

Freeing my hands, I stumble back a few steps. Darion retreats, scoops his jacket off the floor where he must have dropped it and smooths his shirt flat again as he hovers behind Eric.

"When did Brandon cross, Darion?" Eric asks.

Darion raises his eyes to the ceiling and I can see him mentally trying to calculate the amount of days.

"Umm…It took me about a fortnight to get here…I came as fast as I could…He was gone five days when I left. They said they would return him in three. When they didn't, we started to worry. The men voted to send a rider back to inform you. Crossing would probably have led to all our deaths."

He's right. If the Outsiders were angry - by the sounds of it, they were - then crossing would have been the worst idea. The poor man cowering behind Eric is just the unlucky sot that drew the short straw and had to come tell me what happened. But what was Brandon thinking? Crossing the border alone and after having knowingly tried to deceive these people, it was a death sentence.

My brain goes into overload. I shove past Eric and bolt to the door, tearing it open with such force it crashes into the wall and bounces back at me. I'm halfway down the hall when I hear the echo of a half dozen feet storming after me.

"Alistair, stop!"

Eric is yelling and making grounds on me. I ignore his pleas to stop and head to the main hall as I pick up speed. I wind down the spiral stairs, taking them two at a time, the thumping of my boots echoing in the open foyer below.

Bursting through the main entrance to my castle, I break out in a run toward the stables. I have no concern that my council will keep up, being a group of much older men. Regardless, I will not be stopped.

How could I have been so damn foolish? Why did I listen to them? I knew in my gut it was a bad idea for Brandon to go north and a worse idea to have him try to deceive the Outsiders, but no one would listen to me, not even Brandon. They were all so convinced this was the best and only solution. Now Brandon is in grave danger and is deep in enemy territory.

The cold wind cuts through my thin shirt and tousles my blond hair, blowing it in my face. I have allowed it to grow longer than I like and I swipe it from my eyes while I run.

As suspected, my parade of followers has been reduced to just Eric and Darion. Eric continues to yell after me, but I ignore him as I continue at a full sprint to the stables.

The sky is gray and the clouds look heavy with more snow. The winter snows have been endless this year and not a day seems to go by when we aren't being hammered with more inches of the shit. The air bites at my cheeks and I instantly regret my hasty departure and wish I'd had at least the forethought to grab a jacket. Fueled by anger and worry, I hadn't actually felt the cold until I was within sight of my destination.

At the stables, I slide open the barn door and head to the back where my horse is stalled. I glance through the other stalls as I pass, getting a few lazy looks from their inhabitants as I search for the stable hand, knowing he must be around somewhere.

"Mitchel?" I yell as I continue my scan.

A young lad of maybe eighteen, with flaming red hair and lanky, unproportioned limbs pops his head out from a stall farther down. He startles at seeing me and rushes to address me proper, only it's clear he isn't quite sure what "proper" is with me. If my situation wasn't so dire, I may have found the act comical. My unorthodox way of handling my position as King tends to confuse most everyone, especially the unsuspecting commoner like poor Mitchel.

"Saddle my horse. Now."

I turn and glance over my shoulder as the kid rushes to do as I command without question. Eric's broad frame slips through the barn doors at the far end and stomps toward me, cheeks flush from the cold and eyes dark and determined. Darion must have given up, because he does not follow him through.

"What are you doing, Alistair?"

"You know damn well what I'm doing."

"This is a bad idea, you can't-"

"No. You know what was a bad idea, Eric? Brandon going north and trying to be me. *That* was a bad idea. Brandon crossing the border alone and unarmed. *That* was a bad idea as well. You all convinced me it was the best plan, but I knew in my gut it wasn't right. I knew it was dangerous and now Brandon could be dead." A wave of fear washes over me at hearing my own words and I close my eyes briefly to center myself. "I should never have agreed to this. I'm going after him and you aren't stopping me."

"Alistair, wait. Let's sit down and look at the situation. Let's think of the best way to handle it without being hasty and making rash decisions."

"No, Eric. This time we're doing it my way. I'm going and you're not stopping me."

I turn and make my way to my horse where I help Mitchel secure the saddle in place by buckling the straps on one side. I then move to adjusting the stirrups, ignoring Eric's overbearing bulk hovering over me, waiting for me to cave. It isn't going to happen.

"Fine." Eric says with a huff after I shove past him and move the other side to help Mitchel. I'm surprised he gives up so easily. "But you can't jump on a horse and just go without some preparation. Look at yourself, you aren't even dressed to ride. It's freezing out there and the nights are bitter cold. You'll freeze to death, if you don't starve to death first. Spend a moment getting a few things together."

Yanking the saddle strap snug on the other side, I cringe at Eric's words. He's right, I can't just ride away like this. If I ride hard, even throughout the nights, it will still take at least ten days to get to the border and I can't go without sleep or eating for that long, not to mention my damn nipples are already hard as rock and aching from cold under my stupid, flimsy, thin shirt.

I hate giving Eric the satisfaction of being right, but under the circumstances, I have no choice. Leaving Mitchel to finish with the horse, I turn back to Eric and narrow my eyes.

"Have things prepared for me while I change. Keep it to a bare minimum, I don't want to be weighed down. Do you understand me?"

"I'd rather you don't do this, son. I'd rather you think about it first. You have an entire realm to think about. You shouldn't-"

"You will not stop me, Eric. I'm going. Now, have my things put together and be back here immediately. Do not waste my time."

He nods his head and I shove past him to head back to my rooms to organize some clothes and change into my riding gear. I try not to think about Brandon and what could have happened to him, could be happening to him. The thought that he has been killed niggles at my brain. I shove the idea away as far as I can and don't let myself go there. If I lose Brandon... I shake my head. No. He's alive and I'll get him back.

* * *

Fully geared for a long ride, layered for warmth under my riding clothes, I make haste back to the stables. Mitchel has my horse outside and is busy strapping on packs of gear while Eric stands to his side, holding another pack. There is a second horse saddled and standing behind mine.

You stupid bloody bastard! You honestly think you're coming with me? Ha! Think again.

I set my jaw and stomp toward Eric, ready for a fight. There is no way in hell I'm allowing him to come. Eric may be a fit man for mid-fifties, but he pales in endurance when compared to my twenty-seven years and nothing is going to slow me down.

"Forget it," I say as I near him, "You aren't coming."

Eric turns to me as he hands the second pack to Mitchel to strap onto the other horse.

"I'm not, but you aren't going alone-"

"Darion just rode hard to get here, he'll never keep up with me, Eric. I need to do-"

"Let the man finish, ingrate. If you think you're riding out of here and across the realm alone, you have another thing comin'."

I spin around and see Ferguson Harris securing his riding jacket and scowling at me through his thick black beard. Fergus is my first officer, Captain, and best friend.

"And by the way, Jordan is pissed at you too for thinking you were doing this alone. She'd probably be ripping the flesh from your skin right now if she could have left the house, but with a wild one-year-old tearing around and an uncomfortably huge, pregnant belly; I'd say you're safe…for now. But, I don't put it past my wife to kick your ass later. So, get on your bloody horse, quit your whining, and let's get the hell out of here. Shall we?"

Fergus coming with me I can handle. I sneer at him and turn a dark gaze back to Eric.

"You think he's going to stop me going after him?"

"Probably not, but maybe he can talk sense into that stubborn ass brain of yours where I can't. Listen to him, you're not thinking straight right now. You're letting your heart lead you into a dangerous situation."

"I'll send word when I can." I say as I mount my horse.

"Be careful, Alistair. Not a single person agrees with what you are doing. Don't do anything stupid." Eric says handing me the reins.

"I'll keep him in line, Eric." Fergus says as he mounts his horse beside me.

Once the two of us have guided our horses to the main road leading out of the city, I give my horse a firm kick and pick up the pace.

"Keep up, fen-sucker, or I'm leaving you behind."

I'm wasting no time. Brandon's in danger and he needs help.

Chapter Three

Brandon

The tent where I'm being held is shadowed in the fading light. When I was brought in earlier, I observed it to be one of the smaller ones in the encampment, surrounded on all sides by much larger, more elaborate looking ones. It may be dwarfed, but it is the heavier guarded one.

There is a number of woven straw mats overlapping each other and covering the majority of the half frozen, dirt floor. The mats surround a small, low burning fire which sits in the middle of the small tent, venting out of an opening above me. Two iron hinged, red wood chests sit locked off to the side of the entrance and a half dozen emerald and gold silk covered cushions have been provided for my comfort. I refuse to sit on them. I may have come willingly and therefore am not bound, but I will not make myself comfortable here. I'll do what needs to be done and be gone. Hopefully.

The chances of walking out of here on my own free will are non-existent. A dozen guards surround this tent where I'm being held and they have been given strict instruction to not allow me to leave. So I wait. I pace and wait for the man himself to make his appearance.

Their encampment is positioned only a couple miles from the border and from my observation, when I was escorted in, there are easily five thousand men - soldiers mostly - posted around the area. I was watched by many as I was taken to this tent in the middle of it all and the looks I received were far from friendly or curious, they were hostile and angry. I'm the enemy and I'm in their territory. The only prospect of getting out of here alive lies in the hope that this leader is a reasonable man.

I pace the small enclosure and gnaw my bottom lip in contemplation, weighing my options. The rendezvous at the border fell apart. Somehow, they knew right away that I was not who I claimed to be; not the King of Edovia. The men sent to escort us were furious. The terms we had been given and agreed upon, clearly stated that Alistair was to accompany his men for the exchange.

Doing everything in my power to try to talk the enraged group of men down and renegotiate an acceptable truce that wouldn't end up with blood being shed, I managed to convince them to take me alone to their leader. A single man going willingly would show our desperation in needing this peace between us. It was a move I didn't have time to think through and now, alone in this tent on the other side of the border, I wonder if I've made a huge mistake.

Stripped of my weapons and dragged along through the pass, I wound up here in a tent. Alone. Waiting to make audience with the man who leads the Outsiders, the one they refer to as "The Master". I have been waiting the better part of the entire day for his arrival and my nerves are near shot.

Alistair is going to be furious when he finds out what I've done. With any luck, I will be back across the border in the next few days, with or without an agreement and he will just have to huff a lot of hot air when he hears about this and get over it. What else was I supposed to do? Too much was riding on this for us walk away or to stand by and allow ourselves to be slaughtered.

Maybe it was a hasty decision and Alistair will feel the need to discipline me somehow, but I'm sure I can make it up to him. I do not look forward to hearing the "I told you so" remarks he will prate on about to the council after this, but I guess it was coming. He was right. If things go south however, we may be too up to our necks in a bloodbath for any of it to matter anyhow.

I sigh and try not to think that way. I made a rash decision I know, but I have to work with it now. Getting home and back to Alistair is my number one concern. Right after I figure out a way to negotiate our freedom. I can't let myself miss him right now or it will distract my thoughts and I know I can never think clearly with him on my mind. Being away from him has already been hell, but I can't let myself dwell on it; not right now anyway.

A rustle of a flap being drawn behind me has me raising my head from my stewing to meet with the iridescent, pearl black eyes of someone I have not yet met. The man stepping into the tent is tall and slim, lavishly dressed in silver embossed silks of the same midnight black as his eyes. His skin is the color of pale, washed out violet, his hair a darker extreme of the same color reminding me of the flesh of an eggplant. It is long and braided back behind his head, falling to nearly his waist. His ears are oddly long and are decorated with an uncountable number of silver rings on both sides.

I stand to my full height of six feet and still need to raise my eyes to meet his. Is this him? Is this the man who has tormented our lands for all these years? He's not the monster my mind has been picturing. Apart from the obvious differences, he looks like an ordinary man.

"What shall I call you, stranger?" He has a strange accent that makes him draw out certain vowels when he speaks and it takes me a moment to make out what he says.

His eyes drill into my own, full of menace and intimidation and for all the fear I'm feeling, I try desperately not to let it show.

"Your name." He repeats.

"My name is Brandon Leeson, Captain of his majesty's armies in the land of Edovia."

No sense lying now, I've already been called out on my deceit. I give the man before me a respectable bow and wait as he proceeds to examine me.

He walks around me, eyes trailing up and down my body in a way that makes me feel exposed and vulnerable until he is in front of me again. His ominous dark holes for eyes meet mine. He stands a little closer than I'm comfortable with and I have to make a conscious effort not to step back.

"You can call me, Rovell."

I give the man a nod.

"We have much to discuss, Brandon." The drawling "o" makes my name sound odd on his lips. "Firstly, your King made a mockery of my demands and for this reason, I already question if we can come to any agreeance."

"You are mistaken, Rovell. The King would be standing here right now if I had allowed for it, but his council and I would not permit him to follow through with your demands. He is our King and our leader and the risks to him were too high. If you want to place blame for betrayal, you blame me."

"Blame you? A mere soldier. A Captain…"

"Appointed tactical advisor to the King. I could not allow him to come."

"Advisor? Ahhh yes, I see…and?"

"And?"

His eyebrow quirks up as he waits for more. What more does he want?

"And what? I don't understand. I'm his tactical advisor and his Captain."

The man harrumphs and motions for me to join him in sitting. I hesitate, feeling confused, not wanting to become relaxed with this man and let my guard down. However, I suppose if he wants me dead, he will have it that way regardless and I won't be able to stop it.

Lowering myself to my knees, I keep distance between us and an eye on Rovell at all times. I figure the more I can keep the man talking the more I may learn and if I get out of here, the more information I can bring back home with me. If I'm lucky, I can negotiate the truce we were sent here to make.

The man who calls himself Rovell, strokes his smooth, hairless chin and narrows his eyes at me. A smile curls his lips.

"Tell me about yourself, Brandon." Again, my name sounds awkward on his lips.

"I would think you would be more interested in my people and why I'm here, than who I am."

"You are wrong. You intrigue me. You have crossed into my lands, unarmed and with no guarantee of your safety or survival and yet you appear fearless before me. My own men show me more fear than you are right now."

"Your men are cowards."

"Indeed. And they should be. I am a man to be feared, Brandon." He smiles.

"You don't scare me. If your intention is to kill me anyway, then don't waste my time. If you are interested in speaking terms, then let's cut the horseshit and talk."

Rovell watches me intently and rises from the mat. He draws back the flap covering the entrance to the tent and speaks to a man beyond in a language I don't understand. Returning to the mat, he kneels across from me.

"Do you keep servos in your land, Brandon?"

"We don't. It was done away with over a hundred years ago."

"A shame." His lips purse and he watches me intently before continuing. "I have asked for my personal servos to be brought in. He will bring drinks for us, then we may begin a discussion into what has brought you here."

I nod and sit in silence, waiting. My gaze shifts around the small tent and I avoid making direct eye contact with Rovell who is clearly staring a hole through me right now. His gaze is unsettling and seems to have a way of making me feel stripped bare. For all my effort to remain calm and unintimidated, I fear I am failing and he will see I've begun to tremble inside.

Moments later, a younger man, easily no more than twenty years old, with the same hue to his skin and darkness to his eyes as Rovell, enters and sets a brown jug and two mugs on the mat by the fire. The man bows deep to Rovell before standing, making his lithe frame straight as an arrow in front of him, dark eyes staring blankly ahead. His hair is cut short, a lighter hue than Rovell's and carries hints of cobalt in places where the fire light reflects on its silky strands. This man has no rings in his ears but instead has four tiny loops of silver pierced into the left side of his bottom lip.

With no more than a glance, Rovell communicates with his servos and the man moves to kneel beside Rovell, yet behind him by at least a foot. The servos folds his dainty hands in his lap and continues to stare ahead as though we are not even present in the tent with him.

Rovell tips the jug, filling both mugs and offers me one. I accept it with a steady hand, gripping it tight in my fist and bring the mug to my mouth, dampening my lips with its contents. The spicy smell of copper and cloves tingles its way into my nose, stinging my nostrils, while the tang of metal hits my pallet. It is far from pleasant, but I accept the taste and drink a little more; willing it to stay down. I try to hide a shudder and set my mug back on the ground, breathing through my mouth as the thick film and retched taste clears.

"Sodvial Mestormigan," Rovell says in way of explanation, which means nothing to me. I assume it might be what the drink is called. I only nod as I steal a glance to the still figure peering off into an unknown distant vision only he can see.

It's a far cry from whiskey and I can feel the effect of my head spinning from just the one gulp. This stuff can be dangerous and I err on the edge of caution before taking anymore. As much as I'd like a means of steadying my nerves, I don't want to become incapacitated.

Rovell drinks deep and tops his own mug up again before continuing. He seems somehow resilient to its effects.

"Let me be blunt, Brandon. I care little for your people and their survival, they are merely in the way of what I need."

"And what is it you need, Rovell?"

The man pauses, watching me.

"We are very different, you and I, Brandon."

"I made no claims that we are the same. What is your point?"

Depositing his drink beside him, Rovell leans back on his heels with his chin up. "The survival of my race is dependent on a nutrient found in the soils of your lands, of this continent. Where I am from, across the Great Sea, the lands do not produce what we need fast enough to maintain our growing numbers and I was sent forth to discover new worlds and find sustenance elsewhere."

"Your race is dying then?"

"Not anymore. Not for hundreds of years now, maybe thousands. Maybe never. The lands we have claimed on this continent already will keep my people going for centuries more."

"And yet you still plan to take more than you need and take Edovia as well? Sounds greedy."

Rovell chuckles and smirks as he tilts his head at me. "It is my plan, yes. Owning the continent, taking what we need, leaves less risk for my people when they are brought here. It is not greed. Your people would only pose as a threat."

"If you see us as hostile, we are only that way because you have made us so."

"Your people pose a risk."

"Hardly, and you know that."

"Nonetheless." Rovell shrugs and reclaims his mug, spinning the liquid inside.

"So in your mind, the obliteration of my people is the only answer? You've already decided, haven't you?"

Rovell doesn't speak, he lifts his mug and watches me while he drinks deep. His penetrating gaze has me so unnerved, I try not to squirm.

"My being here is a waste of time, isn't it?" I'm convinced I'm being toyed with until it suits the man to kill me outright.

"Before I saw you, Brandon, I was certain no negotiation could be made, but now…"

I catch a hint of movement in my peripheral vision, but when I looked the servos is as still as ever.

"I've changed your mind?"

A smile creeps onto his face as he lowers his drink once again, setting it down.

"We may be able to reach an agreement, Brandon. In fact, I'm convinced of your determination to save your land and your people. Perhaps, you are willing to work with me?"

I quirk an eyebrow at him, wondering where he's going with all this. "That's why I'm here."

His eyes darken more than their pitch black and the haunting smile remains on his lips as he nods his head to my untouched drink.

"Please, have a drink with me. You are tense and we cannot discuss anything proper until you relax some."

Hesitantly, I reach for the mug and raise it to him, acknowledging his request and bring the mug back to my lips, drinking a few mouthfuls of the tangy liquid inside, showing the man I'm agreeable. As I drink, my eyes move back to the servos and

I question in my mind if there isn't a hint of fear that has shifted onto his face. I try to ignore the sinking feeling in my gut.

The aftertaste of the drink bites at my tongue and I scrape it across my teeth trying to rid myself of some of the bitterness.

"What nutrient?" I ask, taking a chance that maybe I can gather some information.

"I do not think there is a word in your language to describe it."

"What does it do then? How do you get it out of the soil and how do you use it?"

"Curious man you are. So many questions."

"If we are to speak terms, then maybe I need to understand your needs so I can sympathize and we can work through this."

Rovell chuckles. "Brandon, let me explain something to you before we continue. My people have secured enough nutrients in the northern part of this continent to last us a few hundred years. In that time, the soils of our home lands across the Great Sea will have replenished to a point that my people will return and leave these lands to do the same. I have no need to claim Edovia, except to secure safety for my people. If I decide to move south, it will be for no other reason than that. Security."

"Than what is it you want from us? How can we settle this with you and have you leave us alone? Tell me, Rovell. I came in search of freedom for my people. What can we do to obtain that from you? How can we give you the security and reassurance you need? Or are you telling me it's fruitless?"

"It's not what your people can do for me, Brandon. It is what *you* can do for me."

"Me?" My heart beats harder in my chest at the twisted riddles he is spinning.

"Yes, only you can bring peace to your people and their lands."

"How? Tell me what you want?"

"The answer is simple, Brandon. You are what I want. You stay here with me. Become my servos. Become one of us. Give yourself to me willingly and your people will be free." Rovell pauses and leans forward, narrowing his beady eyes at me with a look that sinks into my soul. "Refuse me, and I will destroy everything you know and love."

Regardless of the drink I had only moments ago, my mouth and throat become instantly dry. The thundering drum of my own heartbeat in my ears is the only sound in the room and I can feel the hairs over my entire body rise in unison.

Everything appears to become frozen in time. There is no movement and no sound outside my racing heart in my chest.

What do I do?

Rovell's words race around inside my head. The meaning clear. Breaking free of Rovell's hypnotizing gaze, I peer to the servos behind him. The once stone face man has gone pale and his eyes are wide with fear. No longer staring into space, the man - who now appears much younger - shifts his eyes to mine. He's practically a child, not a man. I was mistaken. He is but a teenager of maybe eighteen.

"Brandon. You have my terms. I need a decision." Rovell's words are like shards of ice stabbing into my ears and being scraped across my skin. The air in the small tent becomes thick, almost palpable and I struggle to take my next breath.

The boy's eyes glisten as I watch him. They brim with tears and his jaw tightens as he makes every effort to maintain form.

"Will you take your place as my servos, Brandon? Will you free your people?"

A single tear breaks free from the dark pools of the boy's eye when I speak. I can't look away.

I'm sorry, boy.

"Yes. I'll be your servos."

The boy doesn't even have time to react as Rovell moves with unexpected speed. A flash of iron catches my eye and the next I know the boy's head is thrust back and his neck is split open, spilling his life to the matted ground.

I steel myself not to react. I expected this and as his life's blood pulses out of him, splashing me and puddling on the floor, I watch the dead boy's single tear continue to roll past his chin and fall to the pool below.

Chapter Four

Alistair

It's past midnight when Fergus pulls his horse up beside me. The temperature has dipped even lower than the bitter cold of the daylight hours and my body is tense and sore from having spent so long trying to keep warm while sitting atop my horse and not moving around.

"If we don't give our horses a break and water them, we'll be walking north by tomorrow because they will be dead from exhaustion." Fergus glares at me, waiting for a response. "Do you hear me, Alistair? You need to sleep and eat something too, you can't keep going like this. Besides, I'm freezing."

Ignoring him, I kick my heels into my horse to urge him to speed up, but am rewarded with a snort and only a few paces of a faster speed before he slows again under me.

I hate to admit Fergus is right. We have been riding hard since morning and I'm so weary I've had to fight to sit upright for the last few miles. The cold winter night has my teeth chattering despite my riding coat and I can't seem to get warmth back into my boots any longer and my toes are frozen stiff.

"Come on, Alistair. We can't ride straight through, get that through your thick, stubborn ass skull. Take a break already, we can head out again at first light."

Letting out an audible, dramatic sigh, I tug on the reins to slow my horse to a stop. I slide down from the saddle and stand a few moments, trying to get my feet beneath me. My legs are like jelly from the long ride and as the blood flow returns to them they begin to ache. Giving them a few shakes, I try to work the muscles loose and then begin unstrapping my gear.

Glancing over at Fergus, I see he is wasting no time gathering broken logs and sticks from the surrounding white forest and is stacking them to make a fire.

The trees are heavy from the fallen snow and the ground is littered with the branches that could no longer take its great weight and have broken and fallen throughout the long winter.

I pull my sack free and toss it on the ground near the growing pile of kindling. I make a job of getting a fire lit and leave Fergus to put some food together while I go tend the horses.

The traveler's road runs near parallel to the Clemistine River which is a great asset on long journeys, providing a constant supply of fresh water and fish when needed after a long day's ride. Taking the horses through the woods, the high moon lighting my way, I follow the sounds of the trickling current and let it guide me through the night to my destination.

Using the heel of my boot, I break away a large patch of ice at the edge of the water, enough for the horses to quench their thirst and to fill mine and Fergus' skins. My body shudders as a shiver radiates through me. The temperature has dropped significantly since sundown and the deep winter chill sinks numbingly into my bones.

The horses lap lazily at the water, clearly having no idea just how damn cold I am right now and how desperately I need to get back to the fire and try to work some kind of feeling back into my body. Every extremity has officially gone painfully numb. Even the hairs inside my nose are frozen and sticking together at this point and the saliva in my mouth is frothing.

Back at our makeshift camp, I settle in front of the raging fire to warm my frozen body. I find I have no appetite and instead pull a flask of whiskey from my bag. Taking a long pull of the cool tangy liquid, I revel in the burn as it runs down my throat. It warms my insides in a way the fire doesn't touch and just the smell of it is enough to calm my ever raging nerves.

"Eat something." Fergus says as he hands me a few strips of dried meat.

"I'm fine."

It's the first we've spoken since he declared we should stop for the night. He knows I'm angry, frustrated, upset, and about a hundred other emotions that have me down right cranky at the moment. But, he also knows that I'm stubborn and will never admit to being hungry.

He is right and I hate the man for it. He's always been able to read me like a book and doesn't put up with my attitude for anything. It's the main reason we have been friends for so long. I don't intimidate him and he doesn't take my shit. He tells it like it is and never tries to skirt around issues with me. Honest and straight forward; a royal pain in my ass.

"You can't not eat, Alistair. You have no idea what we are riding into. You need to keep your strength up."

I glare at him and rip the meat from his hand, making a display of taking a huge bite and munching on it with exaggeration so he'll let up and leave me be. He ignores my immature mockery and takes the flask from me, tipping it to his mouth.

"I know you're worried about Brandon, but it's no reason for you to be a complete prick."

"He could be dead."

"Or he could be working that brilliant ass brain of his and be sorting out all those negotiations we planned. He could be working miracles over there for all we know."

"Or he could be dead."

Fergus nibbles on his dried meat and stares into the fire. He knows I'm right. Nothing has gone as planned and the fact that Brandon went over the border alone only paints awful images into my brain. The "what if's" are endless and the hollow, sickening feeling in my gut is back. I toss my last bite of meat into the fire and pick up the whiskey instead. I need sedation not nourishment right now.

"If they've hurt him." I say through a lump in my throat. "If he's dead, we are going to war, Fergus. This will be it."

Fergus meets my eyes and his silence says everything.

"We'll get him back. If he's alive, Alistair, we will get him back and bring him home."

I nod and stare into the flickering flames of the fire. Brandon is my whole world, without him, I wouldn't know how to breathe. The idea of losing him is more than I can take. I can't think about *ifs*. I have to believe I'm not too late.

"What are your intentions when we get to the border?" Fergus asks tentatively. He regards me wearily as though he's finally asking the question that's been on his mind all day.

"Did Eric tell you to keep tabs on me?"

"Of course he did. You're hot headed. You act on impulse and you forget to think. He's right. You are running in there with your heart and not your damn head and you'll get yourself killed that way."

"By the time we get to the border, if he hasn't been returned, it will have been nearly the full turn of a moon or more. I'm crossing that damn border, Fergus, and I'm getting him back. And if I find out that they have killed him…Maker help me, I will-"

"You'll what? Rage on them? You and a measly twenty-five men? Give your head a damn shake. They'll slaughter you. Eric's right, you're a bloody idiot sometimes, that's why I'm here. You need a more solid plan than that."

"I'm crossing alone."

Laughter bursts from Fergus. "Like hell you are. If we cross, we go as a group and we plan every step along the way. We account for every conceivable outcome. We cannot enter as a threat and you are most certainly not going alone."

I know it is a fruitless fight and that no amount of convincing will sway Fergus into changing his mind and allowing me my solo trip, so I drop it and go along with him, for now. If I can calm the beast in him for the time being, maybe I won't end up being tied to a tree to keep me put later when I decide to defy him.

"Fine. What is *your* brilliant plan then since you seem to know everything all of a sudden?"

Fergus inhales deeply and gets up to toss a few more branches onto the fire, stirring it up and making the flames grow.

"You need to be prepared for the very real possibility that we could find out Brandon is dead and if we do, you need to be able to hold your shit together so we can work through it. One outburst and you could risk all our lives. This is bigger than just you. You have an entire realm to think about."

His words send a chill down my spine and this time it isn't from the cold air. I squeeze fingers into my eyes and push away the horrendous images trying to make their way back into my mind. I really don't want to face that possibility at all, the sheer thought is making me sick to my stomach. Although I will never say it out loud, Fergus has a point. If I find out they have killed Brandon, I may come undone.

"Alistair, I know you're worried. I'm just trying to be realistic. Brandon is a smart cat. If anyone can turn a situation around and make it work; it's him. I think we will need to force these negotiations, insist we meet with this leader, and try to do what we set out here to do. In the process we'll find out what happened to Bran...with luck we'll get him back."

"They'll agree to see us. It was my absence that caused this mess. I'm who they wanted at the border for the exchange. If I'm willing to show my face and talk to them, it will show integrity on our part. I'm going over, Fergus. I have to. Do not try to stop that."

"How will you handle bad news?"

I can't answer him. I keep my eyes trained on the fire and drain more cool whiskey down my throat. No amount of drink is helping ease my jumping nerves. The only thing that will make the constant jittering through my bones stop will be having Brandon back in my arms. The idea that I may never feel his touch or smell his sweet essence again almost sends me into an all-out panic attack.

I clutch at my chest and draw in slow, measured breaths trying to remain calm. I'm clearly displaying a lack of control to Fergus already and it's the last thing I need.

Fergus lets out a deep sigh. "I'm sorry I'm pushing you, I just need you to consider it. I won't stop you joining the men, but be prepared, Alistair. That's all I ask. There are a lot of lives at stake. We'll sort out the details when we meet up with the others."

I nod absently, drinking again from the flask. I need the oblivion it offers.

Fergus doesn't discuss the matter further. We sit in silence awhile until my eyes become heavy and begin to droop. My head nods on my shoulders with the weight of a thousand stones and the tug of exhaustion draws my body to the ground. I pull my wool blanket around me and lay my head on my pack. As tired as I am, sleep does not come easily and I swim on its surface, fighting with my subconscious mind for a long while before I am submersed in its depths.

More than once through the night I'm torn from terrifying nightmares of Brandon being tortured and killed and I wake in the darkness covered in a cold sweat. Every time, Brandon's gray eyes implore me to help him, but no matter how hard I try, in the dream, I can't get to him fast enough. I remain helplessly just out of his reach while I watch him die before my eyes.

Giving up on sleep, I rise to stoke the fire and bring it back to life. I watch Fergus, rolled up in his blanket, snoring softly and hope the man won't be too angry with me when he finds out his plan won't be happening the way he intends it to happen. I'm not risking any more lives. This time we do things my way. The way I see it, the realm will be safer if I deal with it alone.

Looking around me, I search for my flask of whiskey and find it buried under my blankets with me. I let out a quiet chuckle; it's not the first time a bottle of alcohol has shared my bed. Maybe not as smooth as a lover's touch, but it certainly has the ability to sedate and warm me. I remove the stopper and tilt my head back draining the rest, disappointed that only a mouthful remains. More to distract my mind than anything, I pull my pack onto my lap and root through it looking for more.

"Consarn it! You bloody, stupid bastard!"

Fergus groans and rolls over, furrowing his brow. "Hell you got a mouth on you, what's your problem?"

"That fen-sucked prick only packed me one bloody flask of whiskey? Is he insane?"

Fergus' laughter cuts through the quiet night. "You're getting soft, castle boy. Since when do you let other people do shit for you. You didn't pack your own bag?"

"I was in a hurry."

"Serves you right." Fergus rolls away from me and draws his blankets over his head.

"Do you have any?"

"Nope." He mumbles.

Great, like I wasn't already on edge. I toss my empty flask at Fergus, hitting my mark and pinging him off the head.

"Ouch, what the hell? Prick."

"Get your ass up, we need to get moving. I'm not sitting around anymore."

Fergus tosses his blanket off himself in a flurry and storms to his feet. "I swear to the Maker himself, Alistair, if they don't kill you across that border, I just might."

Fergus shakes out his blanket and makes a job of rolling it up to be strapped to his horse. His anger at me is evident in his sharp movements and exaggerated grunts. I don't care, I'm in no mood to sit around when I don't know what has happened to Brandon. I just need to keep moving. I can't be idle any longer.

Fergus and I ride long and hard every day, covering many miles and resting only when absolutely necessary. As the days pass, our horses become more weary and my mood is sufficiently less than tolerable. The long days and nights we are putting in has caused our pace to slow considerably. My mind drifts to Brandon a lot. We fought so hard to get where we are today and the thought of him not being there anymore has my world turned upside down.

Chapter Five

Brandon

Alistair's teeth clamp down on my lower lip before he sucks it into his mouth and dives his tongue deep into the back reaches of my throat. I groan against his aggressive domination and thrust my hips up to rub my hard cock with his. His hand slides down my thigh, cupping a firm hold on my ass, pulling me closer still. Our skin together is hot enough to burn. Every part of my body is throbbing in anticipation, wanting to have Alistair inside me, riding us both to climax. I throw my head back and whimper with desire as his teeth find my nipple and bite down, teasing it seductively with his tongue. I can hardly take it anymore, I need more, I need all of him and I say as much. I run my hands over his naked body wanting to feel every inch of him when a thunderous bang rivets through my bones and my eyes pop open, leaving the fog of my far too realistic dream as nothing more than a distant memory.

"You are dreaming of him."

The drawling vowels and rich, deep thrum of the voice leaves no doubt in my mind who has woken me. I lay still and unresponsive, my heart hammering in my chest as I measure out the situation.

Him? Does he know who I'm dreaming about? How can he, it's impossible.

My back is turned to Rovell, leaving my facial expressions yet unseen and I force myself to gain some control as my reality sinks back in.

"You will soon forget this man who makes you call out in your sleep with desire."

Shit! Am I talking in my sleep?!? What does he know?

Another thud, much like the one that blasted me awake, makes me jump. My brain being more alert now understands the noise to be that of the chests lids being dropped shut. The chests that were moved with me to my new tent and that have remained locked, their contents a mystery. I hear the clinking of keys and know Rovell is securing them once again.

"Turn to face me, Brandon. I find your avoidance bothersome."

Shuffling to sit up, I keep the furs I have been given drawn around my body. I turn to face Rovell, keeping my eyes purposefully averted.

"Look at me."

His voice is stern and I raise my head to comply. Our "arrangement" dictates that I do not go against his order for any reason, and I have agreed to his terms. I steel myself as I look in his eyes, determined to hide all emotions from my face.

"Who is he?" He asks.

"I don't know to what you are referring."

"Do not lie to me! Lower your furs."

Keeping my gaze on his dark stare, I bite the inside of my cheek as I remove the warm furs, sending a shiver over my skin as the cold air hits my heated flesh.

Rovell's eyes trail my body and come to rest on the tented, thin fabric of my breeches covering my still hard cock. The only remaining evidence of my lost dream.

"This man, the one who makes your prick stand so rigid while you sleep, will he miss you? Do you love this man?"

"How do you know I'm not dreaming of a woman, maybe a wife?"

"You take me for a fool. Do you love this man you have left behind?"

I grit my teeth at the idea of Rovell knowing anything of my past, especially of Alistair.

"My life before is inconsequential, I'm one of your people now. I am your servos, Master. You should forgive my unconscious mind; it's having trouble catching up."

Rovell chuckles under his breath as he turns to add wood to the low burning fire.

My new tent is much larger than the one where I was originally held. "Fitting for the servos to the Master" I am told. The floor space is at least triple in size, yet the furnishings are sparse. The same woven type mats cover the floor space, only I have been provided with rugs of thick snow beast furs that have helped to keep the cold from seeping through the ground and into my bones. The bedding I have been given consist of some of the most plush pillows I have ever felt, adorned in silken, moss green covers with silver stitching up the sides. I have also been provided with two large furs to help keep me warm. It is wretchedly cold even with them. I have been given little else. Food and drink when required and a basin of warm water to wash daily; "Rovell does not like his servos smelling like scum" I'm told.

"Your constant avoidance of my questions is remarkable. They were not wrong about your brilliant mind."

"They?"

Rovell shakes his head. "No matter." He kneels on the other side of the fire across from me and stares from downcast eyes. I recognize the look in them. The dark pools invade my soul and I find myself inadvertently drawing my furs back up around my body as though he can see right through me.

When Rovell makes no move to leave and I realize I will probably not get a chance for more sleep, I oblige him and join him at the fire.

Squatting down, I keep my fur tightly wrapped around me, hiding my body. I may not have been here long, but long enough to know my limits with the man. Long enough to know my place. I may be able to avoid certain questions and keep somewhat aloof, but I have also learned to obey those silent commands for company, and this is one of them.

"Why have we remained camped here?" I ask. "I agreed to your terms six days ago, yet we remain at the border. I don't understand."

"You will understand in time."

I study the dark pits of his eyes. "You assured me my people and lands would be safe."

"And they are. I'm an honorable man, Brandon. I keep my word."

"Yet you seem to have an ulterior motive."

Rovell chuckles again and uses a stick to stir the fire. Despite the venting in the roof of the tent, the smoke lingers around us in a thick, suffocating cloud and my lungs burn with every breath.

"I will be sending you new attire. It has taken some time in acquiring it, but it should be arriving today. Something more suited to your position here. I want you comfortable, Brandon. If there is anything you desire, please just ask."

I want to go home. But I gave up that right and I know I will never leave. I saw what happens to a servo when their services are no longer required.

I nod and stifle a sarcastic laugh as I drop my gaze to the fire. The man is clearly no more willing to divulge information than I am and the redirection into my "new role" has me feeling uncomfortable. I try to fix my features so he doesn't see my vulnerability. It has taken more than a firm resolve to keep up my end of the bargain and an even harder battle of wills to do it without giving outward signs of my revulsion toward the man.

Who could have guessed the leader of the Outsiders was such a sadistically, creepy man? It's almost mind boggling. No one back home could have predicted this if they'd wanted to.

Rovell stands unexpectedly and draws my attention from the flickering flames. My heart instantly goes into my throat as he stares down at me with an unreadable expression in his eyes, as though he is deciding something. When he moves to the entrance of the tent instead, I let out a breath. *Thank the Maker.*

"I will return in a while, Brandon. I have things that require my attention just now. Do try to rid yourself of this somber mood. I expect you to be completely compliant when I return. No more evasiveness. I am losing my patience rather quickly and you do not want to see me angry, Brandon. When I ask a question, I expect you to answer it. Remember our deal."

I nod and watch as the man's face turns up in a smirk before he makes his way from the tent. Only when he's gone do I allow my body the shiver it has been holding back.

Tears sting the back of my eyes as I bite down hard on my lower lip. I need to work harder at not upsetting this man. He claims to be true to his word, and I want to believe him, but one slip up and I could anger him to the point that he may withdraw on our agreement and Edovia, and everyone there, would be nothing more than a memory.

I close my eyes, forcing my tears away and let the warmth of the fire work its way over my body. It can't touch the bone deep chill inside me. That feeling won't be so easily quashed.

With Rovell gone, I take a moment to reorganize my thoughts. My dream has me off balance and then with Rovell calling me out, it only made it harder to focus and keep my wits about me.

I close my eyes, reliving the invigorating feelings the dream brought with it, if only for an instant. I can't allow myself to go there any longer. I wish my mind would quit reminding me what I have sacrificed.

Alistair will be the hardest part of my past to let go of and dammit if his face isn't forefront on my mind every time I close my eyes. Damn my treacherous heart for holding on so tight. The mere thought of Alistair sends an ache straight to its core and I fight to shed the feeling, willing it to stay numb. Even if I could go back, nothing would ever be the same; Rovell has made damn sure of that.

I drop my head into my hands and scrub at my face. Rovell is slowly tearing me apart. I can feel it. With every ounce of strength I have, I try hard to keep myself together and not let the man take from me what I have spent years building up. But with each passing day, my barriers crumble more and more and the man's poison seeps into my soul, taking me back to a place I long ago tried to forget.

I take solace in the thought that the man will eventually tire of me and have me killed like his last servos. I welcome the day and can only hope it comes sooner rather than later. Accepting his offer, was in turn the acceptance of my inevitable death. It was the letting go of everything I spent so long building. Someday another man will come along who will capture Rovell's interest and my fate will be a reflection of the young boy's from only six days ago. I'll wait with baited breath for that day to arrive.

Alistair's face comes to my mind again. His warm smile with those gorgeous, irresistible dimples; I never could resist those dimples. The shine of his crystal blue eyes, always full of such passion and determination.

He wants freedom for his people. He tries so hard to be the righteous King and do what he thinks is best. I want to give him that much at least. I want to give him the freedom he longs for. He will be remembered in history as the King who saved Edovia. Will he forgive me and what I chose to do – what I had to do?

The man never knew the whole truth about me; about my past. Our lives together had become so comfortable I resigned myself to the fact that I probably would never tell him. I don't regret staying silent about it. Some secrets are best untold. He will move on. He will do better than me. I was never worthy of his love anyway; he just didn't know it.

Rovell was right in choosing me. Only, what Rovell didn't realize is that I'm already scarred deep inside and you can't truly break what was broken long ago.

Pulling myself to stand, I let the fur fall to the ground and stare down at my body. The thin shirt and breeches covering me do nothing to block out the cold and I shiver involuntarily. My clothing covers a hard soldier's body; firm and muscled from years of training. It was not the life I was born to live, but the life I chose when everything in my past went terribly wrong.

I hold my hands, palm up and follow the lines on their surface to the calluses just below my fingers; more indications of the life I didn't deserve. I should never have tried to improve on a life that I wasn't predetermined to live, because now I have to let that life go and I can't keep dwelling on it.

If I can rid myself of the hope I built up, make my mind understand that I deserve no less than what I was given as a child, then Rovell will have no power over me and I can soar through my remaining days unscathed and welcome the end when it comes.

Chapter Six

Alistair

In the early morning of our eleventh day on the road Fergus and I can see smoke and make out the shape of tents in the distance. We are a few miles from the border and are coming in sight of the original negotiation party's camp. The view of our destination causes my heart to pick up in my chest. An underlying fear has been following me our entire trip. It tickles up the back of my neck and sends my stomach to be constantly flipping about. Right now, the turmoil in my gut is at its peak.

What if they know more? What if they don't? What if I'm riding into bad news?

Maker, please let Brandon be okay.

I steal myself for what is ahead and dig my heels into my tired horse, spurring him on. Our poor animals gave up on anything even resembling a speedy trot days ago and we cover the last mile to our destination at a slow crawl.

As we approach camp, my soldiers stop what they are doing and gather. The uncertainty and pity I see in their eyes should be enough explanation, but I allow my gaze to search from man to man as I look for answers, information, an update, anything. The blank faces staring back at me say it all. These men have no answers. A single man among them shrugs his shoulders and shakes his head.

"We've had no word, Sir." The man chokes out, then looks to the ground as though he expects me to be angry at his words and lash out.

They know nothing more than Darion knew. My heart drops and I look to Fergus in defeat.

"Better nothing than bad news." He assures me. "Come on, let's get something to eat and discuss where to go from here. We'll get the information we can from these men and form a plan so we aren't rushing in and doing anything stupid."

I know he's right, even though instinct wants me to spur my horse into the mountain pass in the north and cross the border without a second thought.

I nod and swing down from my horse handing the reins to one of my soldiers who has come forth to help. Fergus orders a few others to put food together and clear a tent for me, as though sleep is somehow top on my list of things to do. Not likely.

The men stay at arm's length, taking orders from Fergus and avoiding interacting with me at all costs. It's evident to everyone that what has taken place has me edgy and unapproachable, but what I can't stand is the bloody pity in their eyes.

Ignoring Fergus' pleas that I rest some, I make my way to the larger fire built in the center of camp and worry my fingers through my new beard as I think.

The warmth radiating off its flames brings feeling back into my half frozen body. I watch the men around me work and feel the tension blow past in their wake as they move around me. No one knows what to say and everyone is going out of their way to keep busy and avoid talking to me. It's for the best. I'm worried and extremely irritable right now. The last thing I need to do is go off on someone.

Having finished whatever it is he was doing, Fergus comes to join me.

"I told you to get some sleep."

"Since when do I take orders from you?" I snap without moving my eyes from the dancing flames before me.

"Tomorrow we're crossing and you need to be with it, Alistair. I need your head in this and right now you are running on empty. For Brandon's sake you should rest."

"I'll be fine."

"I doubt you could piss in a straight line if I asked you to." He mumbles under his breath.

"Suck it, ingrate. I said I'm fine."

Fergus sighs and holds his hands up in defeat. "All right. So I've spoken to a few men and I'm going to pull the rest together and get them caught up. Tomorrow, we all make our way through the pass to the mid-point, unarmed. We'll rally there and send a single rider through to draw their watch to us. On their approach, we will remain still and unthreatening. *I* will request audience with this Master or whoever he is. You keep your damn mouth shut and let me do the talking. I will make sure they know who you are. You're right, your being there might make them more willing to accept us. From that point, we play it as it goes. We draw as much information out of them as we can and hopefully they allow us the meeting. But I beg you, Alistair, let me do the talking and whatever we learn about Brandon, you hold your shit together. If you're not careful you could get us all killed."

I half listen to Fergus as he goes over *his* plan with me. What happens tomorrow will be my decision in the end, and Fergus won't like it one bit, because his brilliant plan is nothing more than wasted breath. I hold my tongue, knowing if I let him in on my idea now, he will just spend all night trying to talk me out of it. I know the risk I'm taking, but my mind will not be swayed.

Fergus continues to trek on through the possible outcomes and how we can deal with them if they arise; I tune him out. The overthinking and over planning is giving me a headache and none of it matters. Finally, he goes off to get all the other men on board and leaves me in peace.

As night settles in, the men in camp head off to bed in anticipation of our day tomorrow. Fergus gives me another lecture about sleep before he turns in as well and finally a peace settles in around me. No one else has bothered to speak with me today, each man feeling partly responsible for Brandon's absence and not wanting to rock the boat.

As I rub my stiff fingers together and hold them out in front of the flickering flames trying to work out the cold that has settled into my bones. A brave soul, one who has yet to head to bed, dares to come and stand beside me.

Doctor Chase Schuyler joins me, standing silently at my side, staring mesmerized into the fire. His presence has always left me confused and full of conflicting emotions. This is the first man Brandon ever loved. Even though it was years before him and I got together, a rooted jealousy still lingers somewhere inside me, refusing to let go. I spent a long time hating this man, wishing he'd never come into my life, but then, without really realizing when, a respect for him grew over the last year and now I hesitate to call him a friend. All I know is he is certainly no longer my enemy.

Chase shuffles beside me and wraps his arms around his body, hugging himself. I've often wondered what Brandon was drawn to when he and Chase were together. Chase is a much smaller man than either of us, maybe a generous five foot ten at most and his small frame, long, brown hair and green eyes are the exact opposite of the six foot, heavily muscled, blond haired, blue-eyed me.

Shaking my head, I try to clear the quandary that always confuses my mind. I bring my thumb to my mouth and tear again at the raw skin that is trying to regrow from the days and days of abuse my teeth have been giving it since news arrived in Ludairium.

"I tried to stop him." His voice is soft when he speaks, and I can hear the lacing of fear around his words. It is not me he is afraid of - at least I hope not, I don't blame him - but for Brandon and where he has gone.

"What happened?" I ask. If anyone is going to give me the truth of it, I know it will be him.

Chase shakes his head and sighs. "They knew. I don't know how, but it's almost like they anticipated we'd send someone else and not you. They didn't even consider that Brandon was you for an instant."

"I can't sort this out. It just doesn't make sense." I pause trying to reorganize my thoughts. "Darion said he went willingly?"

"He did. Brandon didn't deny the truth when they questioned him. He admitted to who he was and that the risks of sending you were too high. They were going to turn around and refuse any talk, return to their leader and tell him of our deceit. You could see their hostility mounting. It was turning ugly, fast and I think Brandon could see that if they went back across and reported what we'd done that it would mean the end for us. So Brandon told them to take him and him alone to their leader."

I cringe at hearing what Brandon did. The clamp around my heart tightens and I lower myself to sit on the ground by the fire, not sure if I can keep my legs beneath me while I listen. Chase joins me, squatting at my side.

"Brandon told them he would go willingly and unarmed as a single solitary person to meet their leader, no party to join him. He would be of no threat to them. He convinced them and I tried to stop him, Alistair, I did. I swear to you, but he wouldn't listen to me. He said he had to try. He couldn't bear what might happen if he did nothing. We were sent here to make peace and that is what he was going to do. It all happened so fast and there wasn't time to talk about it or consider any other options. One instant we were losing ground to an irate bunch of Outsiders the next, Brandon is laying down his weapons and…" Chase's words drop off and he stops speaking.

I turn to meet his eyes and for the first time notice how tired and red they are. He looks like he hasn't slept in days and I know I must look the same. Chase still cares deeply for Brandon. He wouldn't want to see any harm come to him any more than I would.

"They said three days?" I ask, not sure if I understood Darion correctly, seeing as I was in a flurry to get out of Ludairium the moment I heard the news. I never did clarify this point with him.

"When they agreed to take him, they told us their leader would speak to him within two days' time. We assumed he may not be nearby and needed to be informed and brought to the border. They said Brandon would meet with him and be returned to us. Dead or alive. They made no promises. They said it would be the Master who would decide. All previous assurances were void, therefore no guarantees were made. The men explained that if their Master agreed to hear him and terms were met, we could probably expect him to return in about three days' time, but..."

Chase trails off.

"It's been more than thirty days."

Chase nods. "They haven't delivered us a body. Alistair, he's still alive. I know he is...but..."

My stomach turns and if I had any food in it to throw up, I'm sure it would have come out. The shaking rattling through my body and the fact that I have eaten minimally since leaving the city makes it hard to think. The only thing I know for certain, is I'm going over that border and I'm getting my Brandon back; no matter the cost. This is the only thread of hope I've been given that he might still be alive. It's not much to hold on to, but it's better than nothing.

I blow out a breath and try to regain some control, Chase is watching me and I hate to appear as though I'm falling apart, even though I'm certain I am.

"You are going alone, aren't you?" Chase says.

I look up to meet his eyes, their green depths dance and shimmer in the light of the fire.

"That's not the plan."

"It's not Fergus' plan, but it's yours isn't it?"

I scan the camp to see if anyone else is awake and about. We're alone and at least thirty feet stand between us and the closest tent.

"I forget how damn intuitive you can be."

"You're kind of an open book sometimes."

I huff out a humorless snort of laughter. "Am I?"

"I'm sure I don't have to tell you to be careful and I'm sure Fergus has already lectured you endlessly on your way up here…"

"You have no idea. The guy can be a right pain in my ass."

"He's alive, Alistair. I know he is. I feel it in my gut. Bring him back."

I nod to Chase and look into his worried face. The flood of jealousy is back when I see how much he still cares for Brandon. There is love in those eyes, even if it's just the love of a friend and not a lover any longer, it's there and I see it. I rein back the urge to become angry and remind myself what Brandon always tells me. Chase is a part of his past, but I am his future. I smile inside thinking of just how many bloody times Brandon has had to remind me of that. In fact, I can hear him scolding me right now, reminding me of how much he loves me.

"I saw Aaron a few days ago, before I left the city."

Chase's head swings back my way and his eyes widen in anticipation of what I have to say. Aaron is another reason I no longer need to be jealous of Chase, and right now I selfishly need to see Chase's enthusiasm for another man and erase the sorrow he was feeling for mine.

"He's still slung up and following doctor's orders. Begrudgingly. He claims Dr. Greaves is being hard on him and he feels much better and should be on the field."

A soft smile passes over Chase's lips. "Sounds like Aaron. Eager to jump back into things and unwilling to sit still."

I nod silently watching the flames dance in the darkness. Aaron is one of my newer soldiers, joining my ranks less than a year ago. Him and Chase began a relationship right before he marched north with the negotiating party and just after an unfortunate accident that left Aaron with a broken arm. I knew Chase was probably worried about him, so it's nice to be able to give him a taste of home. Even if it isn't much.

Rising from the ground and stretching my weary muscles, I peer down to Chase. "Do me a favor and keep your mouth shut about my plans until morning. Fergus is going to be none too happy with me, I don't need him finding out prematurely."

When Chase nods, I stumble my way to the tent Fergus had prepared for me. I doubt I will sleep, but I know I should probably try at least. Tomorrow will be a long day.

Chapter Seven

Brandon

I pick at a loose gold thread on the hem of my new robe and watch as it slowly unravels leaving the tiniest holes where the tailor's needle penetrated the crimson silk. I run a finger over the puckered fabric and cringe because I know Rovell will be angry if he sees what I've done.

I was given new attire, as Rovell promised, and going along with our "terms", I did not argue even though I find the new clothes far outside my comfort zone.

A full robe of smooth, deep red silk, delicately stitched with golden thread in an interlocking cubic design around its base covers my body all the way to my moccasin covered feet. It is cinched with a braided, golden tie around the waist. The long sleeves bell out at the end and the scalloped edges fall past my hands. It is light and slides over my skin unlike anything I have ever worn, making me feel naked even though my body is fully covered. I'm becoming more accustomed to its airy, loose fit, but I find it more uncomfortable then anything and bitter cold against my skin.

I pull my fur over my shoulders and continue to pick methodically at the delicate stitching on the bottom of my robe in an effort to keep my mind distracted.

I try to remember how long I have been gone. The days are blurring together now and I'm finding it harder and harder to keep track of the passing of time. Eighteen? No. Twenty? Damn, I've lost count. *Does it even matter anymore?*

If Rovell is a fair man, which I continue to believe he is, then the people of Edovia will be able to continue their lives without the worry of war any longer. If I knew for certain Rovell would leave our lands alone based on the promise he made me, I would have ended my life long ago - after my first day as his blasted servos - but the thought that I would anger him holds me back and instead I have fallen into old habits, pulling further and further inside every day.

He will tire of me soon enough. Then I will be killed.

I refuse to allow myself to remember my old life back in Ludairium and the people in it. That life is gone. I made my choice. I had no idea what might happen after our "agreed terms" were originally met. Would we leave the border and travel north? Would he toy with me for a couple days and then kill me? Rovell has done neither and I don't know what the future brings anymore because so far he keeps me around and continues his games with me and we have remained camped at the border.

Soon, it won't matter, I can feel myself slowly returning to the hollow, empty shell of a person I was as a child. I never thought I would ever return to such a desolate place again, especially after fighting for so long to earn my happy ending. But life is cruel and somehow, I've wound up back on that path, winding down that road I left long ago. Only this time, I won't get out alive.

Men speaking outside the tent draw my attention away from my thoughts. The voices are hushed and they speak in their tongue. I have yet to make out the meaning of any of the words. They talk quickly and it's never intended for my ears, the murmuring too soft for me to piece together. I recognize one voice, it's Rovell's.

I stop picking at the threads on my robe and close my eyes, squeezing my hands into fists, digging my nails deep into my palms, trying to escape. I take a few steadying breaths as I release the tight grip on my nerves, letting my body relax and go to the calm serenity, deep in the pits of my mind. Nothing can harm me here. I'm nobody, nothing, hollow and empty. I surround myself in my own protective barrier and prepare for the metaphorical punches to my soul I'm about to take.

Rovell enters the tent and I look to him without seeing. I rise from my cocoon of cushions in the corner and bow my head as I have been instructed to do and await his commands.

Rovell approaches, raises a hand to my cheek, bringing my head up and traces a thumb across the growth of the beard that I have let grow over the past eight days.

"Why do you insist on displeasing me with this?"

"It's cold, I wish only to stay warm. I'll shave if it angers you, Master."

"If you are cold, I will have more furs sent in. I want this removed. I do not like it." He plays his thumb over my chin and tilts my head side to side as he looks in my eyes. "Why do you look so foreign and sad?"

I remain quiet and focus on the blacks of his eyes, trying to keep any and all emotion from my face, burying it deep within. If sadness is showing, then I haven't dug deep enough.

"Speak your mind, Brandon. Do not ignore my questions."

"Why have we not left the border? You said my agreeing to be your servos would be all you needed to leave my people alone, yet we have remained here."

"Ah, it is worry then that I see in your eyes. You doubt my word?"

"No, Master. I covet your word; you are a most honorable man. It is simple curiosity."

"Hmm…Are you loved by your people, Brandon?"

I close my eyes briefly and breathe steadying breaths through my nose while I fight off images of a dimpled smile, one of a certain blond haired, blue eyed man I use to adore in what feels like another life. I will never go back there. I push it away.

"These are my people now and you are my Master, Rovell."

"Such obedience." Rovell smiles and draws his hand behind my head, threading his fingers into my hair and holding my head in place close to his. "Do you think your people would leave you here, forget about you and not come fighting to get you back?" He asks.

I reopen my eyes and set them on his beady pearls. He's so close, the musky, spicy smell of him invades my nose, but I don't flinch away.

"Haven't you sent word that I will not be returning?"

"I have not."

My mouth gapes slightly before I clamp it shut again, fixing my features. I don't mean to break my composure, but his words throw me off. I assumed word had been sent ages ago that a deal was made and the price of Edovia's freedom explained. If my people don't know…

"How long have I been here?" I ask not trusting my calculations.

"Near on the turn of a moon. I should expect his arrival soon. You are more naïve than I expected, Brandon. A man with as brilliant a mind as yours should have seen my deeper plan by now."

His nose traces up along my jaw bone and I close my eyes again to focus on what he is saying. He is actively throwing me off which he has not been able to do thus far and I'm mad at myself for allowing it. The soft brush of his lips across my ear sends a shiver to prickle my skin under my robe.

I swallow a lump in my throat. "Deeper plan?"

"I never expected you to be mine forever. Only for long enough…"

Rovell chuckles a sadistic laugh as he pulls back slightly to pause and watch me. The release of his hold leaves me standing there, brain a muddle as I try to work out what I've missed. He is still so close and my thoughts are trying desperately to sort through what he is saying.

Who is he expecting? My heart rate picks up and my mind swims as I fish for answers. If word hasn't been sent, no one knows terms have been made and met. They don't know of their freedom. No one knows if I'm alive or dead. No one knows... Anything. *Alistair!* Oh, Maker help me. Rovell will kill him if he comes here.

"You've pieced it together." Rovell says.

I raise my wide eyes to meet his and see him grinning at me, watching my reaction. My skin crawls and I have to fight harder to keep control, but it's slipping away. I need to bury myself deeper. I can't let this man affect me. I close my eyes and shield myself from the situation again before I can look at him.

"I will not kill him, as you fear. You have my word. I have got what I was seeking. He does not know it yet, but the suffering I have inflicted will be carried for a lifetime. It is far more than I could have hoped for." Rovell lifts a hand to my face letting two fingers dance across my lips. "Such a sweet thing you are and who could have guessed you had demons buried within you already. That only helped make my victory more profound."

I don't recoil at his touch, I have disciplined myself better than that and I have shifted my walls back in place.

My face becomes a blank slate and my voice turns steady and flat. "Permission to touch you, Master?"

"Always."

I trail my finger up the length of his arms and wrap them around the back of his neck pulling his head to mine, resting our foreheads together. His skin is cool and clammy to the touch, much smoother than that of most men I have surrounded myself with all my life. An unusual characteristic of their race I have observed.

"I cannot go back. Please, if he comes, send him away. I implore you. I'm yours to command, I understand, but tell me, have I displeased you, Master?"

"On the contrary. This could not have worked out better. We will await his arrival, and soon my whole plan will be clearer." He brushes his lips softly across my own as I remain perfectly still, ignoring their slick dampness and coppery taste.

"No, please, Master." I breathe against his lips.

I cling to his neck tighter and plead with my eyes, pressing my body to his. He reaches up and removes my grasp, holding me at bay.

"Our time together is short, Brandon. Such a shame. I have enjoyed you. You have been a worthy servos."

Rovell drops my hands and goes to exit the tent flap. "I will send more furs and a bladesman to remove that infernal scratch from your face. Understood?"

"Yes, Master. Anything you desire."

Alone once again, I continue to stand, staring into the fabric of the tent closure where he has exited. I never expected to be rescued or to go back. I expected word to have been sent to Edovia that I would never return, or that I was dead. I expected to die as just another one of this man's exhausted servos' one day. Only now do I see, this was not Rovell's plan, hasn't ever been his plan and I was blind to it. How could I not see what he was doing?

My stomach coils and I clamp my teeth down into my bottom lip. The thudding of my heart echoes in my ears and I close my eyes against the rush of panic flooding through my veins.

How can I go back now?

My control is slipping. I can feel it. I need to push away the feelings, the emotions. Why won't they stay where I want? I was so much better at hiding them as a child. I will not panic. I will not fear. I will not feel any of it anymore.

After a few steady breaths, I open my eyes and go to my cocoon of cushions and furs. I kneel among them and draw the pelt around my shoulders again, cutting the winter chill. A low fire burns in the center of the tent, but it is doing little to cut the bitter cold clinging to my body. Sitting with the fur snug around me, I stare deep into the embers and remind myself who I truly am. Who I once was.

I am nobody, I am nothing. I do not feel and I am not afraid.

Rovell can't take from me if it was never there to give. I remember the lost boy I once was. The childhood I left behind so long ago and I make my heart stone.

The new life I created in Ludairium, the innocent man with the strikingly blue eyes, the feelings of love and happiness; it was all nothing but an illusion. A lie. I must forget that life, for I'm not Brandon Leeson any longer. That man is dead. Rovell reminded me who I really am. He managed to resurface the child inside me, the boy I had tried to forget. My name is Jeremy Weston. I should never have thought I could have been anyone different.

Chapter Eight

Alistair

Finding no solace in sleep, thrashing about in the grips of one bad dream after another, I decide to get back up and sit by the fire with a jug - not a mug, that wouldn't be near enough - of ale. Not the same comfort I find in whiskey, but anything to numb my mind is a welcome companion at this point.

My mind is stuck on Brandon and what I may or may not be walking into tomorrow. Negative thoughts keep pushing into my brain and I do my best to keep them at bay, trying hard to focus on a more positive outcome. I try to anticipate having him in my arms again, and kissing his lush lips. I close my eyes and envision making love to him. Maker help me, I'd never known what it was to feel so connected to another person before Brandon. Sex was always emotionless for me and done for the sheer necessity of needing release, but with Brandon it has always been so much more; right from the first day. I discovered what it meant to make love.

Sometime in the night, with visions of Brandon swimming in my head, I fell asleep in front of the fire. This morning, I open my eyes and try to swallow the bile lining the inside of my dry throat. While pulling myself off the cold ground my legs creak and waver underneath me, shaking and refusing to hold my weight without determination. I have gone too long on little sleep and even less food and my body is beginning to protest. Fergus sees me up and scampers over to join me, shoving yet another mug of ale into my hand.

"We need to get this underway, brother. The men need their orders and everyone is too afraid to approach you right now because you're being a miserable prick. Do you want me to start pulling everyone together?"

"No. I need food." My voice is scratchy and raw.

My plan will not be a popular one and I expect all kinds of resistance, especially from Fergus when he finds out, so I'm not ready to lay it all out just yet. I need to eat and get my feet beneath me before I can jump into action. I need to control my racing heart and focus my mind on how I'm going to proceed.

Eating in silence, I feel the men watching me. Fergus is by my side and waits - rather impatiently, while he fidgets and grumbles - until I scrape the last of my porridge from the bowl and swallow it down. I've barely stood when Fergus barrels around to block me from walking away.

"Here's what I'm thinking," he says without missing a beat. "I'm going to rally the men together and let them know what we've talked about, then…"

"I'm going alone." No point allowing him to waste his breath. I pin him with my eyes, daring him to argue.

"No. What? Wait a minute…That's not what we talked about, Alistair." He hisses at me in a low tone as he tries to keep everyone from hearing. Me, I'm beyond giving a shit what people will think right now.

"Actually, Ferg, in case you haven't noticed, I've barely said a word. You keep shutting me down. You've conjured up this wild plan and now *I'm* telling you how it's going to happen, so listen up. It's *me* they wanted, not Brandon. *I'm* crossing alone. Yes. Alone. Without you or anyone else. If he's alive, I'm offering up a trade. Me for him. Have Chase ready in case Brandon's injured and needs doctoring."

Fergus' face contorts into a mixture of shock and disbelief. I can almost see his brain wanting to burst. "Have you lost your mind? They'll kill you." He spits.

"Maybe, but I'm going anyway. It doesn't matter. I need to get Brandon back here safely, so stand aside and cool yourself. I'm doing this."

When I make to move around him, he halts me with a firm grip around my jacket, swinging me back to face him. Not a wise move on his part. I'm tired, I'm cranky, and I'm borderline going to snap.

"Safely? What about your safety? I can't allow you to do-"

"You will not stop me, Fergus." I wrench his hand from my shirt and hold a death grip around it, digging my fingers into him with enough force I'm edging on breaking bones. "As long as I have reason to believe Brandon is alive, I will fight until my last breath to get him back. Do you understand me? If I march in there with twenty men, they will feel it is a threat and it could be the nudge they need to finish him off…along with the rest of us. It's too much of a risk. I go alone. I'm who they wanted. They will free him. I know they will."

"Alistair, we already talked about how we could look less threatening. You need to trust in-"

"It's not up for debate. Saddle the horses. You can ride with me to the pass then I will walk alone from there."

He gapes at me, seemingly unaffected by the pain he must be feeling in his hand. I can only imagine the man he is seeing right now. I've come completely unhinged and must look stark raving mad in his eyes.

"Eric's right. You have your head so far up your ass you can't see straight. You aren't even considering how close we are to an all-out war. You're the bloody King and you're acting like a love sick teenager. He's one man. We have thousands here to protect-"

In one, quick sweep, I release his hand to grab his chin with the same ferocity. Bringing my face to his, I can see fear swim up in his eyes. We've always been equals; because I've allowed it. In this moment, with all fleeting sense evaporating into the air around us, I glare into Fergus' face with cold, hard eyes. I will assert my authority over him if I have to and it won't be pretty. Best friend or not, he needs to back down before he pushes me over the edge and I'm precariously close right now.

"He's *not* just one man. He's *my* man. Do not make me pull rank on you, Captain, because I will and it could get ugly here really quickly." The low reverberating tone to my voice is laced with venom and warning. Daring him to keep this up. "I am not leaving him there to die and that's final."

"And how the hell long do I wait for your bloody body to be returned, huh? What do I do when we have no word again for days or longer?"

I bite back a retort that will only result in fists flying and step away from him, releasing my hold. He's reined back his anger and his words are now only that of a concerned friend.

"Once I cross, send men back to Ludairium to rally the troops. The armies need to march north. We are going to war."

"Alistair-" Fergus pleads, but I can't hear it. I need to remain focused on the task at hand. My Brandon needs me.

"Saddle the horses, Fergus."

I toss my empty bowl aside - I forgot I was still holding it - and storm away.

* * *

The pass isn't wide where it winds through the mountains. It climbs and dips at their base making for awkward travel with horses. Alone and on foot, I take consolation in the cold wind beating against my face and the quiet solitude of the white, mountainous forest all around me.

I always figured marching an army through this narrow passageway would be difficult, but seeing it with my own eyes, I have no doubt it is the primary reason our lands have remained untouched thus far. Not impossible, but bottlenecking an army through here would certainly not be favorable.

My hand falls reflexively to my side in search of my sword hilt that is no longer there. I feel unnerved and half naked without its comforting weight against me. As I walk, my mind races through what I may find on the other side of these white peeks and what I might be walking into. To distract my thoughts, I try to envision Brandon in the way I know him best rather than let the nightmares my brain keeps creating take over.

His dark blond hair falling in waves in front of his face, tickling my cheeks while he laughs, leaning over me on our bed, showering me with kisses. His smoldering, gray eyes whose look alone can see into my soul and know my every desire. His lush, swollen lips, red and raw from a night of endless attacks from my own.

I smile at the memory. I love the way his body reacts to mine when we make love, the way he digs his fingers into my skin, marking me before he lets himself go and calls out my name, uncaring who will hear anymore. Even the flush in his cheeks the next morning when we take our meal and he notices the sly smiles on the maid servants' faces telling him just how many people did hear him in our throes of passion. Every little thing about him still sends butterflies to flutter my insides. But now, the memories leave me feeling empty and hollow inside.

Sending him north was the hardest thing I've ever had to do. It took endless nights of his convincing me nothing would go wrong before I gave in and allowed him to go. Even then, I worked hard to change his mind up until the day he rode north.

"I'll be fine, Alistair. You've trained me well. This will go exactly as we planned and I'll be home before you know it."

His hand that had been caressing my cheek wraps around to the back of my head and pulls me closer. His warm lips press against my own and sends my heart to thud harder in my chest. What if this is all I get? What if this is the final kiss? I kiss him back harder and try to hide the tremor that is radiating over my body.

"Please be safe. Don't do anything stupid. I can't take the thought of not having you return."

"I'll be back before the snow melts."

"Promise me?"

When he remains silent I know it's because he can't and my stomach turns at the implication. Brandon will never make a promise he can't guarantee to keep and this is one of them. Regardless of the confidence he feels, this mission is a dangerous one that could fall apart regardless of all the planning in the world.

"They're waiting for me. I have to go."

I glance to the men and saddled horses awaiting departure. Every one of them trying hard to not watch their King and his lover as they say goodbye.

"I love you, B. You don't have to do this. We can sort something else out. Stay with me here. Please don't go."

"You know as well as I do that we need to do this. I love you, Alistair. We'll end this war. I know we will. Then life can settle down some. Trust me."

With a sigh, knowing I can't win this battle with him, I nod. "I trust you."

With a final kiss that I fear again is my last, I watch him walk to the other men and mount his horse. He carries the appropriate air of authority with these soldiers and I couldn't be more proud.

Sitting tall on his horse, flanked by only the best of my men, I watch as he rides away.

He's been out of my arms for half the winter and I miss him so profoundly, I forget how to function without him most days.

Up ahead, I can see the end of my journey through the mountains. It is near dusk and I have been travelling all day with nothing more than my thoughts to keep me company on the last leg of my journey.

Fergus, having tried everything in his power to convince me not to do this all morning, left me to walk alone at the midway point of the pass. At the last moment, he even threw in my face that it's not what Brandon would want me to do, and he's right. Brandon, if he's alive, will be livid at the actions I am taking.

My eyes catch sight of movement up ahead and I freeze in place, scanning my surroundings. I've been spotted. Five men on horseback ride at full speed toward me, weapons drawn. I spread my arms out to my side and display them palm up, open and empty. I don't want to appear a threat.

The men slow their approach when they are within thirty paces of me and I see them scanning the trail behind me.

"I'm alone," I say, "and I'm unarmed."

The men surround me and I let my gaze fall from one to the next in turn, studying their moves, trying to read for any danger. All my efforts will be in vain if they decide to kill me here on the pass.

They are dressed in a combination of leather and iron plated armor. They don't have the appearance of soldiers; each one of them seems too thin and too lacking in strength to be worthy of a good fight. I try not to let that naïve thinking sink too far into my head. These men have taken every realm in their path without mercy and where they may not have strength, I'm certain they make up for it in intelligence and agility.

A single man drops down from his horse and approaches me, hand resting on his now sheathed weapon at his side.

"Brave man wandering over here alone. Who are you, besides a fool?"

I square my shoulders and stare him down. "My name is Alistair Ellesmere and I'm son to the late King, Chrystiaan

Ellesmere, and ruler of the realm of Edovia. I've come to seek audience with your Master."

The man steps closer to me and I follow him with my eyes, holding his unwavering onyx gaze with my own. The man's eyes are like dark little pits and his skin is tinted violet like a sunset.

I have only heard of other races through stories and fairy tales when I was a boy. To see one standing before my eyes, looking so much the same yet so very different than myself, makes me forget my purpose momentarily while I just stare at him in awe.

"Alistair Ellesmere, King of Edovia." He says matter of fact. "You've come alone?"

I nod.

He harrumphs. "You are late." Spinning around he points to two of the men with him. "Bind his arms. We'll take him to Rovell."

Without pause the two men jump down from their horses and pull my arms behind me where they are tied skillfully with a thick piece of hemp rope. The bindings are tight - too tight - and after only a few moments my fingers start to tingle. I pull at the ropes in an effort to loosen them a bit, but have no success.

I'm pushed along the rest of the way down the pass as the sun makes its way down in the sky. As we crest the top of a final hill, the valley below comes into view and my jaw comes unhinged at the sight before me. I suddenly realize that my armies are no better off than children using sticks as swords when compared to the masses I see before me. Thousands of tents and even more soldiers litter the miles of ground stretched out across the land. If I had to guess, I'd say there were easily five or six thousand troops here alone. Knowing the tactics of war, having studied for years under Eric and the council's hard hand, I know this is only a fraction of his army.

Shit! We never had a chance.

I'm taken through a camp bigger than my own city with hundreds upon hundreds of tents filling every space and thousands of men running about busy at tasks, each and every one of them armed to the teeth. As I'm marched through the bustle, men stop to watch us. I'm noticeably not one of them and their curiosity follows in my wake. Whispers among them are hushed and spoken in a strange tongue.

I'm stopped outside a plain tent, somewhat smaller than the rest, and the men restraining me are instructed to hold me there and wait while the other man, the one who seems in charge of the group, talks with more people outside the tent. I let my eyes scan my surroundings, taking in all that I can see.

The talking goes on for longer than I like, in a language that is foreign to me, and I become antsy, wanting to see Brandon or at least discover what has become of him. The man leading the group finally approaches me again.

"You will wait for Rovell. He cannot see you just now."

"Where is my Captain? The man who crossed a moons turn past with your men. Where is he? Is he alive?"

A smile curls the edges of the man's thin white lips as he draws nearer me.

"Is that why you have come here?"

"I've come to make peace with your Master, discuss terms, and yes, to find out what has become of my Captain."

"He is very much alive and, Alistair Ellesmere, King of Edovia, Rovell has been waiting for you. He will be pleased to hear of your arrival. He has taken quite a liking to your Captain." The man chuckles.

I try to keep my face neutral even though my insides are screaming and raging to know what he means by that. I want to pin the man by his throat and beat the truth out of him, claw at his face and rip that smirk off with my bare hands, but I bite back my words and remind myself to breathe. The thought that this Rovell character keeps Brandon to amuse himself and torture him makes it hard to hold my ground and my tongue. Perhaps binding my hands was a wise decision.

I'm moved to another tent where my legs are then bound to prevent my escape. Where exactly they think I will go surrounded by thousands of men I'm not sure. The hilarity of the act almost makes me mock their stupidity, but again, I clamp my mouth shut and say nothing.

By the time men come to take me to this Rovell it is past midnight and the moon is on it's decent in the sky. My legs are freed and I'm escorted into a tent nearby. My eyes scan the dimly lit space hoping Brandon might be present. The tent is empty aside from a pile of cushions and furs in the corner. My eyes are drawn to a dark mark on the woven mat covering the floor. It is a large stain and I recognize it immediately as dried blood. Swallowing the lump in my throat, pushing the implications out of my mind, I try to keep my feet beneath me. The man said Brandon was alive. However, he made no indication that he was unharmed. Is this Brandon's blood? If so, he was badly hurt. The stain is large enough to make me think a man would never have survived that much loss.

"Sit, Rovell will be with you shortly." One of the men escorting me unties the ropes from my wrists before slipping out the tent flap and leaving me alone.

Free from my binds, I rub at my wrists where the rope has chafed my skin leaving it raw. My fingers tingle and hurt as the blood returns to them.

The space being otherwise bare, makes my eyes remain stuck on that dried puddle on the floor. I edge myself closer and lift the end of the mat to see where the spill has seeped through and the ground below has drunk it up. So much blood. Is this from my Brandon? Shuddering, I drop the mat and scan the room again looking for any other clue that this blood might be his. Beside a low burning fire there is also a tray that has been set aside with a jug and a pair of mugs. Nothing else gives me pause so I pace. My nerves make it impossible for me to relax.

A ruffle of noise behind me makes me turn to see a tall, slender man entering the tent. He has the same violet hue to his skin and a long braid of plum colored hair falls past his mid back. His eyes are the same dark abyss as the other man I spoke with, clearly a trait of their race.

"Rovell?" I ask. I pull myself to stand tall and raise my chin to meet his eyes above me.

A smirk plays across his face. "Alistair Ellesmere, King of Edovia, I am told."

"I am." I do not humor him with formalities and instead stand my ground and glare into his eyes.

"I've been waiting for you."

"So I hear."

"Your deceit at the border was a disappointment. A very unwise decision on your part."

"I understand. You requested my presence at the border and my council felt it too dangerous for me to comply with that request, but they were wrong. I have come to make amends."

"It was not a request. It was a demand and you sent an imposter."

"My Captain. Where is he?" I try hard to keep the emotion from my voice.

The man inhales deeply and moves to kneel on the mat before the fire. A smile tugs at the sides of his mouth as he pulls the tray toward him and fills the mugs.

"Sit. Share a drink with me."

I approach the mat, stepping around the dark stain and kneel across from the man accepting the offered drink without hesitation. I will not give him the satisfaction of showing fear. My mind has been made up and Brandon's safety and release is my only concern.

"I have come to offer an exchange." I say.

The man raises an eyebrow.

"An exchange?"

"Me in place of my Captain. I'm the one you wanted at the border, not him. Here I am. Keep me and let him go back to my people."

"Hmm." He raises the drink to his lips and drains half the liquid from his mug. "Brandon's life is more important than your own? Somehow I do not understand your logic…King."

I hate that he uses Brandon's first name and I hate even more the way it rolls off his tongue. It sends a twitch to my lip that I quickly hide behind my mug.

"The lives of all my men are important."

"What if I told you Brandon has won the freedom of your lands for you? We have agreed to terms and your people are free to live on their own soil with the promise that no harm will come to them. Hmm? What say you then?"

Freedom? Agreed terms? Brandon has worked some kind of miracle. Then why isn't he being set free?

"If terms are agreed upon, then why do you keep him here? Why don't you release him?"

"Bah, he is but one man. Forget him. My men will return you to your lands. Ride away. Don't look back. My people will never step foot on your soil again. You have my word."

"I will not leave him here." My heart beats painfully hard in my chest. "Take me instead."

Rovell's steady chuckle and cold glare grates on my nerves and leaves me fighting to hold my tongue...Again. I have a terrible habit of getting myself in trouble because I don't think before I speak. Not this time. Brandon's life is at stake and I will control myself.

Rovell places his mug down and leans in closer to me, eyes like pits, showing off his dark, evil soul.

"Tell me, Alistair Ellesmere, King of Edovia, why the life of this mere soldier means more to you than your own?"

The smirk, the eyes searching me, his overpowering manner hovering above me, I set my jaw and give him back the same penetrating glare and lower my voice to a whisper. Rage flows through my veins.

"Because I will fight for him until my last breath. Because I will die for him if I need to. Because I love him more than life itself. More than you will ever understand."

As I speak, the smile grows across his white lips and he nods in time with every one of my statements as though he expected them.

"You take me for a fool, Alistair Ellesmere, King of Edovia." My fists clench at hearing him continually repeat my full name and title the way he is doing. "I have been watching your lands and your people for near on two years. I have been watching *you*. I have kept you busy, running across the realm, organizing your armies, as I toy at your cities walls. Nothing but a little game for me, some fun, but oh the panic I have caused. I could have claimed your lands in a heartbeat years ago if I had wanted to - you've seen a mere fraction of my armies - but what fun is there in that. Like I told Brandon, I have no need of your lands. My people have all that we require."

You sick, sadistic bastard!

"And what is that?" I ask through clenched teeth.

"Bah, it is of no more consequence. What I'm trying to explain to you is that I have known for a long time who you are and every aspect of your life. Every. Aspect." He emphasizes with a raised eyebrow. "I have brought you here as a demonstration of my power."

"You didn't bring me. I came on my own."

"Is that what you think?" The corner of his mouth quirks up. "I have your lover. I knew you would come for him. I brought you here simply by having him in my possession. I know your love for him."

"How could you have known we were planning to send him in my place? That's horseshit."

"You underestimate me. Eyes and ears everywhere. Foolish King. You played into my hand exactly as I knew you would. When he is returned to you, you will see what I mean. What I have done will serve as a constant reminder to you of the power I possess. Every day you will see the cost of your freedom in this man's eyes. I could kill you right now. Believe me. But, killing you outright would bring me joy but for one day and pain to you for a mere instant. What I have done to your sweet Brandon will bring you pain every day until you breathe your last and I will have the satisfaction of knowing what I have done until I breath my own."

My fists clench at my sides. "What have you done to him you piece of shit."

The pleased grin on his face brings all the horrific images of what could have happened to Brandon back into my mind. Rovell rises to his feet and turns to leave.

"Come, I think it is time we reunite you with your lover."

Chapter Nine

Brandon

I watch the embers burning in the fire. Their soft orange glow pulses like the slow rhythm of a heart at rest. The colors dance and change from blue to purple, orange to red, and the haze and wavering of the heat play tricks on my eyes.

Whenever Rovell is not present, I either sit here, making my mind nothing more than a blank slate as I try not to think of anything and anyone, or I sleep. I have lost count of the days for all the time I spend with my eyes closed, but it doesn't matter anymore. I quit praying to the Maker long ago when I remembered that the Maker doesn't venture into hell to save lost souls. In this world, I am the damned.

My eyes keep closing as I stare at the dancing flames and I keep being jolted upright when my head bobs, heavy with sleep. The effort to crawl to the pile of fur and cushions that is my bed is too much and I suffer the torture of fighting off sleep a little longer.

Being jerked back to the surface of consciousness yet again, the sound of voices outside my tent wake me fully. The haze of sleep evaporates as I listen, trying to make out who is here.

Within a few short words, before I know who is speaking, the flap of my tent is being drawn aside and Rovell enters. When I see him hold the flap and another person pushes through behind him, my heart speeds up in my chest.

A familiar form from my past life comes through and lands piercing blue eyes on me, concern contorting his face as he scans my person and glances back to Rovell. My cheeks feel cold as the winter air blows in and I watch this man I once knew, now fully bearded as an emptiness fills me. I push the feeling away. Emptiness is something. My aim; feel nothing.

Rovell holds him back when he speaks, not allowing him to approach.

"Brandon, are you all right?"

The deep thrum of his voice wants to soothe, wants to wrap around my withered soul and pull me back from the emptiness. I don't let it. My eyes find Rovell's and I stare obediently at him instead. I cannot watch the pain radiating from the eyes of the other man.

Holding a finger up to the bearded man, keeping him at bay, Rovell's eyes never leave my own as he approaches me.

"I told you he would come." Rovell circles me and stands at my back, so close I can feel the heat of his body up against me. His breath is hot across my neck and his lips trail up to my ear, gently grazing my skin. I don't flinch and stay as firm on my feet as ever, eyes trained on a smear of dirt on the corner of the tent. I know my place. "Are you not pleased to see this man? Are you prepared to leave now, Brandon?"

"I made a deal with you for the freedom of my people and the lands of Edovia. Leaving would break that deal." My voice is hollow and as empty as my soul.

Rovell tsk's at me as he moves his mouth over my earlobe, toying at it with his tongue.

"You see, Brandon, but this is exactly how the plan was to play out. You cannot stay here with me any longer. You see this man?" He reaches around me and grips my chin firm in his hand, forcing my face around to look to the blond haired man from my past. "Alistair Ellesmere, King of Edovia, he is your lover yes? See him? Look at him, Brandon. He needs to be reminded every day from now on of my power and that is now your responsibility. Keeping you here would rob him of that and then maybe one day he would forget."

I cringe at hearing the bearded man's name and close my eyes blocking out the sight of him because memories want to flood my brain. I push them down. I push them away. When I open my eyes again Rovell is before me still holding my chin in his grip.

"You will return to your lands with the knowledge that your people are free. Take with you the memories of your time here, Brandon, and never forget what I have given you." His tongue flicks out and wets the smirk on his lips.

The idea of returning to the fake life I made, of trying to dig my way out of this hole once again seems an impossible task and my vision blurs with unwanted tears. I fall to my knees before Rovell and gaze up at him with pleading eyes.

"Please, Master." Searching his face, I look for some kind of mercy. "I cannot."

"Oh, sweet one, but you will."

"Kill me, I beg you." My words whisper out of me with the air I've been holding in my lungs. "I wish to die."

"But that would be too easy, sweet one."

He pulls me to my feet and traces a hand over my now cleanly shaven face.

"I will send for the clothes you rode in with and you will return to your lands with this man, to your life before. My face will swim in your nightmares, my touch will crawl under your skin, and my words will echo in your mind for an eternity. Every breath you take, will be a reminder of the cost of your freedom and this man, your lover, will spend every day watching your pain and knowing it was me who caused it."

Rovell brings two of his fingers to his lips, kisses them, and places them on mine.

"You will be escorted to the pass at dawn."

Rovell turns to the bearded man who I refuse to name.

"True to my word, your lover is unscathed and your people and lands are free." Rovell snaps a finger and a man rushes in the tent carrying a rope bound scroll and hands it to Rovell. "On this parchment, written in my own blood, is your promised freedom. It may mean little to you, but I assure you I am a man of my word. Your people and lands are your own. I hope we never meet again, Alistair Ellesmere, King of Edovia."

I see the flap of the tent move in my peripheral vision as Rovell leaves the tent and stiffen with the knowledge that I have been left alone with the one man I may never again be able to face.

I cannot look at him. The pain in his eyes will be too much. He's known me too long. I've allowed him to be closer to me than anyone before and he will see into my hollowed out soul and know the truth of my shamed existence. He will see what I have kept hidden for so long. This man has the power to break down my barriers and open me up. If he does that, then everyone will know…Everyone will see.

Brandon's life is nothing more than a lie I convinced myself I deserved, but in truth, I have always been that lost little boy, hiding from the world. I have always just been Jeremy and this man does not know Jeremy.

His movement catches my eye. He approaches me cautiously and reaches out a hand. Fingers grazing my arm. I feel them cold through the silk of my robe and I shiver and draw away from his touch, pulling my arm close to my body.

"B?" He whispers.

He tilts his head to look into my face, but I close my eyes to block him out. I cannot allow him to draw me out. He will see the lie my life was and know I'm no longer the man he fell in love with.

"Brandon? What has he done to you?"

What hasn't he done to me?

The pain in his words sends a tugging to my heart and I have to fight the urge to fall into his arms and weep. I can't. I mustn't.

I'm nothing. I'm nobody. I don't deserve any of it.

His fingers are under my chin, coaxing my face to turn to his. I keep my eyes closed and spin away, shoving his hand from my face, turning my back to him. I keep out of his reach.

I'm nothing. I'm nobody. I cannot feel.

"I'm sorry. I won't touch you. Please talk to me, B."

I swallow the thick saliva gathered in my mouth and open my eyes to stare at the ground.

I'm nothing. I'm nobody.

"You shouldn't have come." I say.

"Brandon, we are getting out of here. By dawn we will be on the road to Edovia, we are going home. It's over, B."

"It's over." I agree with finality. The man he loved was a lie. He is gone, never to return. He can never love the man I am now.

I'm nothing. I'm nobody.

I kneel to the bed of straw and cushions and grab my fur, draping it around my shoulders. Laying down, I face the side of the tent, closing my eyes against the waking world. I hear him settle not far away. For a long time he doesn't speak and I'm lulled to sleep by the crackling of the fire and the winter wind fluttering the sides of the tent.

Sometime in the night, I'm stirred by a hand brushing my hair from my eyes and I wake to realize I have turned over. I'm facing the fire, my cheeks wet with tears I don't remember crying. He is sitting beside me, watching me and stroking my forehead. I meet his eyes briefly and push his hand away. I turn and draw my fur over my head.

"Don't let him win, Brandon. It's what he wants. You are stronger than this. I know you."

You don't know me.

His voice continues to talk to me about anything and everything. He tells me of how he found out of my crossing the border and his journey north. His voice wants to console me, the familiar deep thrum wants to wrap me up, comfort my worries away. I can't let it. I fight to turn off my ears and block out its mellowing warmth.

In my effort, I succumb to sleep again and my dreams are filled with lies. A past that my unconscious mind wants me desperately to remember and take back, but my waking mind knows cannot be. In my sleep, I cry for the life that has been destroyed and the lost boy that has come back to haunt me.

The rest of the night is fitful and I thrash around trying to fight off all thoughts and bury myself into a dark hole where I can be alone. Nothing. Nobody.

Chapter Ten

Alistair

Hands down, this has been the most painful night of my life. Brandon tosses and turns as I watch him fight off nightmare after nightmare, screaming out in his sleep, crying, thrashing, and whimpering my name. Every attempt to comfort him so far has been met with flailing arms and when he awakes, he keeps me at bay, throwing off my attempts to soothe him. My heart has never felt so much pain.

Stirred from another horrifying nightmare, Brandon turns a tear streaked face to mine in confusion before his reality clears in his mind and he shows his back to me yet again. I stay kneeling beside him, hands in my lap, my own tears at seeing his pain burning in the back of my eyes. I wish I knew how to help him. I wish he would talk to me.

"If I didn't think it would cost us both our lives, I'd kill that man with my bare hands. I swear to you, Brandon."

He remains silent, his gaze turned away from me, eyes swollen from the tears he shed as he slept. My heart breaks seeing him so distant and in such anguish. Rovell's price for our freedom is becoming clearer the longer I sit and watch the man I love suffering. My once strong, unbreakable soldier, full of determination and love, has been shattered under Rovell's hand.

Once he has slipped back to sleep, I move cautiously and trace my hand up his arm to his face and very carefully stroke the hair from his eyes to caress his wet cheeks. He looks so small curled up beside me and I want nothing more than to scoop him up in my arms and hold him until all his hurt goes away.

"No matter what happens from here, I'll be by your side, B… Always." I whisper.

* * *

As promised, Rovell shows up at dawn with a group of men ready to escort us to the mountain pass.

The instant Rovell walks in the tent, Brandon trips over his feet as he scurries over to the man and falls to his knees before him. The tears fall in waves down his cheeks as he implores him.

"Please, Master, I beg you, have mercy and end my life. I have done all that you ask, can you not see it in yourself to do what is just?"

His words tear at my heart. I can't understand why he doesn't want to come back with me. The way Brandon bows to Rovell, the way he speaks to him as though he has been reduced to nothing more than a slave, drives my anger home and I'm nauseated by the scene before me and bite back the words that want to fly out of my mouth.

Rovell's face lands on mine and a sickening smirk curls his lips before he reverts his attention to my begging lover at his feet.

"Stand, Brandon. It is not becoming for you to beg."

Brandon shuffles to his feet, seeming awkward in the fancy attire Rovell has him wearing. His eyes never look to me, only stay fixed on the man before him as he shakes his head.

"I cannot go back. Please. Have mercy-"

Rovell places a finger to Brandon's lips before caressing his cheek. It takes everything in me not to slap the hand away and take the man down where he stands. The anger at what he has done to Brandon consumes me and I use every ounce of self-control I have left to at least get us out of here alive.

"Hush, my sweet thing. You know that is not part of my plan. This anguish you are feeling, this need to have your life ended and not face your lover, only tells me I have succeeded in my mission. I have no more need for you and you will not die by my hand or the hand of any of my men so quit begging for me to end your life. You will return to your lands and endure the suffering I have instilled in you."

Brandon grabs at the hand on his face and holds tight to it, his eyes go wide with panic.

"No," he pleads, "don't do this…"

Before he can finish speaking Rovell's other hand flies up and strikes Brandon across the face, sending him stumbling backwards. He trips on his feet when they get tangled in the robes and he lands on his ass beside the fire.

I jerk forward at this outburst of violence on Brandon, but am stopped by the tip of Rovell's dagger at my throat, pressing into my skin. The man moved so fast I didn't even see him draw his weapon.

"I would not if I were you."

I shift my eyes between Brandon and Rovell and hold my hands up in surrender while I take a step back. Brandon sits slumped by the fire, a hand to his face and a distant look in his eyes.

Rovell's eyes never leave mine. He sheathes his weapon and snaps a finger. Six men enter the tent and stand at attention awaiting instructions. Rovell walks the few paces to me and sneers.

"Brandon will need to change. My men are prepared for your escort. Be gone from here and do not return, Alistair Ellesmere, King of-"

"Listen, prick." I stay back, but refuse to leave without saying something. "You're wrong. Brandon is stronger than you know and he will come back from this. He will come back to me and I swear on my father's grave, if I ever see your face again, I will kill you."

Rovell chuckles in my face and I clench my fists, resisting the urge to hit him.

"I admire your courage. Safe travels, King of Edovia."

He turns and leaves.

* * *

Six men escort us to the midpoint of the pass. They keep our arms bound as a display of their power, because honestly, where do they think we will go? The leader of the men is the one who unties us before setting us free to walk the rest of the way back to Edovia on our own.

Getting in my face, a move I loathe from anyone but especially these people who I have come to hate even more, he draws his lips back over his teeth sneering at me.

"If you or any of your people cross this path again, you will be killed on sight. No questions, just death."

His breath is rancid as he speaks and I pull back, crinkling my nose. I don't doubt what he says, and I have no intention of testing his warning.

The man mounts his horse and rides off with the other men back down the path to their camp that is now out of sight. I watch them ride away in the distance and when I'm certain they are gone, I turn to Brandon. He has fallen to his knees and is sitting back on his heels, head drooped down, hands in his lap.

Approaching cautiously, I kneel before him. His eyes are closed and his cheeks are flush with cold. I reach a hand to his and he instinctively draws away. My heart seizes in my chest.

The man I sent north is in bad shape and I'm scared to death Rovell's words may be true. I don't know exactly what the man did to my Brandon to cause him to be so withdrawn and anguished, but my tormented brain has a pretty good idea of the possibilities and those thoughts alone make my gorge rise.

I rest my hands in my own lap instead, mirroring Brandon. He does not raise his head even though he knows I'm here. I sit with him a long time saying nothing, just watching him. His lip quivers every now and again and I see him fight the urge to take it in his teeth and gnaw on it, a habit I've seen him do a hundred times before when he is worried or anxious. One that makes me want to draw him into my arms and comfort him. I don't.

The morning slowly passes and I know if we don't get moving soon, we will not be back to camp before nightfall. I chance running a finger over his knee to get his attention.

"Let's go home, B."

He doesn't respond, but his eyes open and he watches my finger graze his leg. It's the first time he hasn't swatted me away. The tension in his body is clear in the rigidity of his muscles.

"B, you're free of that man and this place. Our men are camped a half days walk from here. We can be there by nightfall. Please." I offer out my hand. He doesn't take it and instead closes his eyes again, blocking me out. I let out a huff of air and drop my hand again. I take in our surroundings and try to think of how I can get him moving.

I stand up and pace away from him a bit, watching him, looking for some sign that maybe he is thinking about this and will eventually get up and come with me on his own. As time continues to pass, I see it is not his intent.

In front of him again, I chance touching him, thread my fingers through his hair and stroke at his head. He doesn't pull away, but I see him flinch. The connection feels good and I wonder if maybe I can slowly bring him around this way. One careful touch at a time.

As I'm about to settle back on the ground in front of him, Brandon moves unexpectedly making a grab for my leg. Hooking my foot, he shoulders into me sending me flailing backward. Confused, I land with a hard thud on my ass; jarring my elbow and sending pain to zap right through to my fingers.

What the hell?

Brandon's hands are groping at my boots on both sides and I kick him off, trying to squirm away.

Realization dawns on me, he's looking for the bloody dagger I ordinarily keep strapped to my leg.

"Stop it, dammit! I don't have one." He locks his body around my leg, clinging on as his hands rips at my breeches, digging around. "Brandon, for crying out loud, I'm clean. Do you really think I'd go over there armed?"

Brandon shoves away from me in a huff and stands. He storms off in the opposite direction and I fly up off the ground and go after him. I know he's been through hell and I know he's in a bad place right now, but he is beginning to piss me off. Where does he think he's going? If he walks back toward their camp, they'll kill him…

Oh.

Idiot, that's what he wants.

I grab hold of his arm and spin him around to look at me. He pulls at my grasp and when he sees I'm not letting go, he plops himself back on the ground.

"Consarn it, Brandon! Get your ass off the ground and get moving before we freeze to death out here. Quit playing games."

Frustration sizzles inside me, I yank at his arm trying to force him to his feet. All I manage to do is drag him along the ground as he pulls against me. Fighting against each other, him pulling one way, me the other. We are getting nowhere. Defeated, I drop his arm. When I let go, he falls to the ground and curls up into a tight ball.

"Bloody Hell." I say under my breath.

I swipe a hand over my face and rub at my eyes. I can't even remember the last time I slept properly. I'm beyond tired and my nerves are sufficiently frayed. Dammit all to hell! I have to get Brandon moving one way or another before I snap. I take a deep breath, trying for calm and kneel beside his crumpled body. His face is buried in his hands and I peel them away. The moment he feels my touch, he thrashes against me.

"Stop it, Brandon!"

I'm starting to think it might just be easier to knock him out and drag his sorry ass back to camp. I use all my strength to roll him on his back. We are pretty evenly matched in strength and it takes my determination to win over his to finally flip him over. I sit on him and pin his arms underneath my legs, taking a firm hold of his face so he will look at me.

"Listen to me and quit fighting."

The energy drains out of him when he realizes he can't move. His eyes glaze over and he stares through me instead of at me. I loosen my grip on his face and try to calm myself down. I don't want to be angry with him and I don't want to force my hand with him, the man has already been through enough, but I do need him to listen to me and get moving.

"Listen to me. Quit fighting. I don't know what happened to you over there, babe, but Maker help me, I'm not your enemy."

Babe? I've never used any term of endearment with Brandon before in the year and half we've been together, but somehow it rolls off my tongue like it is the most natural thing ever to say. He flinches at my use of it and regardless of the empty stares, I know he hears me.

"I don't have to touch you or talk to you, but I need you to go with me. If you don't go on your own power, I will drag you kicking and screaming, I promise you. The only way you will stop me is by knocking me out and I don't honestly believe you want to hurt me, do you?"

Brandon's breathing becomes more rapid under my weight, subtle tears pool in his eyes and his lip quivers. He turns his head from me and I know I'm getting through to him.

My heart aches to take away his pain and I'm moved to take a risk. I draw his face around and pull his head up to my shoulder and hug him, burying my face in the crook of his neck. He doesn't return the embrace, only lays still under me as I hold him, trying to take away all his hurt in the simple gesture. When I pull back and rest his head back where it was, I can see the wet streak of where a tear has fallen down his cheek.

"I love you, B. Please come home with me."

I rise off him and hold out a hand to help him up. He stares at the sky above and I'm momentarily afraid he isn't going to move and I will have to take a more drastic approach.

Ignoring my offered hand, he rolls to his front and slowly pulls himself to his feet. Without looking back, he moves along the pass toward home. It is a small victory, but a victory none the less.

Chapter Eleven

Brandon

With sunset comes the night chill. My breath frosts with every breath and cold creeps under my jacket and over my body, despite our steady pace. I can no longer feel my fingers and make failed attempts at pulling my coat sleeves down lower to cover them.

Camp is close and although thoughts of warming my hands over a hot fire should appeal to me, I'm only filled with dread at walking back into a life I willingly abandoned.

Alistair has kept pace with me all day, remaining a respectable distance behind me. I know he is watching my every move and that fleeing is not an option, however desirable the prospect of getting away from it all is.

Being near him is dangerous. Every time I allow his fingers to touch me in any way, he manages to break down a little part of me; exposing the hurt and pain and threatening to draw me out. I can't let him. I can't be the person he wants anymore. The man he knew was not real and the man I truly am deserves nothing, especially not his love.

As the moon makes its slow climb in the sky, and we come out the other end of the pass, distant campfires come into view. Almost simultaneous with my discovery of camp comes a sharp whistle that pierces across the darkness. I can hear men yelling and scampering about, as they group us and watch our approach.

I stop dead in my tracks for the first time since I finally decided to move earlier today. Alistair is instantly behind me, looking over my shoulder.

"They've spotted us coming is all, let's keep going."

He rests a hand at the small of my back and I stiffen at the contact as it sends a warmth to crawl up my spine and seep into my body.

"Come on, B. You've come this far. We'll get something to eat, warm up by the fire, and try to sleep some."

A few men in the distance are approaching. Their murmuring grows louder and I see them draw their weapons, having yet to determine if we are who we are and not Outsiders.

Alistair lets a sharp whistle of his own out, a signal to our men that it is us and not a threat. The men sheathe their swords as a single man breaks out of the cluster of men running full tilt toward us.

I let my gaze fall to the ground and close my eyes.

When I was a child and thing got to be too much, I would close my eyes and try to picture myself in an entirely new setting, far away from the reality I was in. The solitude helped me to accept my surroundings without fight. It was always some place secluded, like a lake or a meadow. I would picture birds flying over rippling waters, diving for their dinners, doing their damnedest to get the elusive fish below or watch as deer grazed the long grass with their fawns close beside them. I would imagine the warm breeze of summer blowing over my face, rustling my hair. It made my heart more peaceful and if I worked on it and created more detail, it managed to wipe away the horrors that had enveloped me.

I picture that place right now in my mind. I try to create the smells of the fishy water and the feel of grass tickling my bare feet. Crashing waves and birds calling to the heavens.

The entire vision is ripped away when large hands grab me into a tight hold, embracing me. Blasting from my peaceful escape, I instantly feel as though I'm suffocating and suck desperate breaths of air into my lungs with wide eyes, as sudden urge to flee overcomes me.

"Holy hell, Brandon. We thought you were dead." Fergus says, tightening his grip around me in a rib crushing hug.

Panic floods through me and I scold myself for being unable to hold onto the serenity inside my mind. It's been too long and I was so much better at it as a child. I will need to work on it. I should not be so easily pulled back. I don't want to be here. I don't belong anymore.

More arms are peeling Fergus off me.

"Stop, Ferg. You'll freak him out, he's not okay. Where's Chase?"

Fergus' arms drop away and I suck in deeps gulps of air. The spots that had been forming in my vision disappear and the dark night comes back into focus.

The two men move off to stand a few paces away from me and are talking low. I hear my name and know they are talking about me. My world begins to weigh heavier on my shoulders at the prospect of what they may be discussing. All that I wanted to hide will come out. They will know. The crushing weight of that knowledge makes me turn off my ears as I walk away into the night. Away from them, away from camp, away from it all. I need to leave this place.

My heart thuds in my ears and I match my pace to its steadily racing beat. I don't expect to get far and so when a hand clamps around my upper arm, I'm not surprised and deflate under its pressure. There will be no escape for me. I'm bound to my past and will suffer it for always.

"Come on, babe, you aren't getting away from me that easily."

Maker, no. Please don't call me that. It sounds too good to my ears and creates bigger cracks in my walls.

I don't fight him. There is no point. He has numbers behind him now and any chance of getting away would only have me met with a barricade of men. I shrug away his hold and turn back to walk to camp.

Shame washes over me at the stares of the men I once called friends. I can tell they've been made to stay back. *I don't belong here anymore. Can't they see that? Can't they see I'm not that man anymore?*

Alistair's hand is at the small of my back again and he leans closer to speak in my ear. He's precariously close and I want to step away.

"I'm going to get you some food. Stay with Chase, I won't be long."

The hand leaves my back and his presence moves away. Chase. I hadn't even noticed him near me. I raise my eyes and see the man standing before me, brow scrunched up with worry, arms folded over his chest. His green eyes are filled with sympathy and an understanding only he would know. He reaches a hand up and holds it out to me.

"Come on, let's go sit. You've been on your feet all day."

This man knows. He'll see my retreat to the past in my eyes and my heart sinks. No one was ever supposed to know that part of me, but a moment of weakness, a long time ago, let it out. Chase knows Jeremy's pain. Chase tore that secret from me a long time ago.

I reach up to accept his hand and allow myself to be led to an empty campfire. Will he protect that piece of me? Has he already seen the truth in my eyes?

I stare solemnly into the flames doing my best to ignore the goings on around me, specifically the stares and quiet whispers from the mouths of my former soldiers and friends. Alistair brings over some food and drink and he and Chase have a quiet word together.

Once again, I know it is about me and a shiver runs up my spine making me shudder.

To my surprise, Alistair moves off and joins Fergus at another campfire about thirty paces away, but his eyes never leave me. I can feel their unwavering gaze.

Chase sits down beside me and holds out a mug. I don't take it.

"Alistair says you've had nothing all day. Drink up."

I shake my head and close my eyes trying again to return to the peaceful seclusion of my mind, looking for a way back to the lake inside my head.

Chase sighs and puts the mug down again. He shuffles beside me and I flinch when his fingers touch my forehead to brush my hair out of my face. His thumb traces over the tender flesh of my cheek where Rovell hit me this morning. The sting of his rejection and refusal to end my life still fresh in my mind.

"Brandon. I need to know if you are hurt anywhere else. Did this man beat you, cut you or mark you in any way that may require my help?"

I almost want to laugh. Did Rovell cut or mark me in any way? The question is hysterical in my ears. Chase could search my whole body and he would never find a single indication of anything being wrong, because Rovell was smart with his tactics and has instead left his mark deep within my soul where no one will ever see it. In the one place where it could torment me until the end of time. It is a wound Chase can never fix.

I shake my head at his absurd question. Chase's hand is under my chin, pulling my head up.

"Look at me, Brandon."

I open my eyes and his knowing gaze is on me again. He searches my face, the concern wrinkling his brow ages him years. Chase lowers his voice and runs a finger across my cheek again.

"Maker help me. What has he done to you, Brandon?"

I feel the tears sting my eyes and I squeeze them shut before they give me away. Rovell may have refused to end my life, but he took away my will to live and this in itself is a far worse punishment than everything else I had to endure.

"I can't go back." I say.

Chase's arms are around me and he pulls me against his chest holding me tight.

"Alistair is worried sick, you can't run away from this, Brandon. You are stronger than this, I know you are. Everyone is here for you. You are safe with us."

My heart aches in my chest. Alistair needs to move on without me. I can't return to that life, no matter how much I might want to.

"I need you to eat something and drink, please, Brandon."

Chase pulls away, grabs the mug again and holds it to my mouth tilting it up. The ale hits my lips and I let some pass to flow down my throat. After a few gulps, I pull away and shake my head. It turns sour in my gut right away making me nauseous.

"No more."

"Food now." Chase reaches for a spoon and holds a heaping helping of meat and potato stew to my mouth. The smell hits my nose making me gag, but Chase is persistent and in hopes that maybe he'll leave me in peace after I give in to him, I accept a few bites. When I can't take it anymore, I shove his hand away, turning my face. I have no appetite and the food hitting my stomach, mixing with the drink, is only making everything roil around uncomfortably.

"I want to sleep." I say.

Chase stands with a sigh and waves a hand in Alistair's direction, calling him over with the gesture.

"No." Grasping his arm, I spin him back to me, trying to stop him. "Please, I can't be near him."

Chase squats down beside me, cradling my face in his hand.

"Why?"

I gape at him, my mouth opening and closing and I can't seem to find words to explain. How can I explain without bearing my soul? I can't, and I won't. I let my shoulders drop and I look to the fire again in defeat. Chase watches me for a beat then moves off to meet Alistair halfway. I can't hear what they say. It doesn't matter. Nothing matters anymore.

When Alistair suggests I head to a tent, I go. I can't make him understand any more than I can make Chase understand. The life they want me to return to no longer exists. I can't be that person anymore. The sooner they discover that, the better. For now, I'll just float through each moment and try not to feel.

I am nothing, I am nobody.

My night is fitful and full of nightmares that cause me to wake up in a cold sweat, shaking and unable to calm myself. Rovell has become front and center to them all and I'm convinced I may never sleep a proper night again.

Each time I awake, Alistair is by my side. I'm sure he doesn't sleep, only sits by and watches me. The emotions he wears on his face are unguarded and raw. He is consumed with worry. Again, the tug in my heart envelops me. I turn away from him. He could never love who I truly am, so I must block out the longing I feel to be comforted by this man. I need to do this for him and allow him to learn to live without me.

Chapter Twelve

Alistair

Our journey home is nothing short of miserable. Brandon has reached the point where mostly he doesn't fight, he just complies with whatever demand is thrown his way, except when it comes from me. With me, he bucks everything. He won't so much as look at me, let alone allow me to touch him any longer and I'd be lying if I said it didn't cut me deep into my heart. There is a vacancy in his eyes that unnerves me and no matter what I do, I can't seem to draw him out.

Chase spends a good part of every break we take practically force feeding Brandon. His reluctance to take food concerns me, but I'm grateful for Chase's persistence with the matter. It just seems like one more way he is pulling away. One more way he is shutting down. He has been so striped of the man he was I barely recognize him.

Before packing up our camp at the border, Brandon finally permitted Chase to examine him for wounds. He found none, as I suspected. Brandon suffered something far worse than a beating at the hands of Rovell and the silent glances shared amongst Fergus and Chase tell me I'm not the only one who sees it.

We are a few days ride still from Ludairium and the weather has warmed slightly, enough I can feel the ache in my toes again and can ride without gloves.

During a midafternoon break, leaving Chase to handle Brandon, I head down to the Clemistine River to water my horse and freshen up, but mostly to clear my head and be alone. Not surprisingly, Fergus is hot on my heels. He's been grilling me for information since Brandon and I crossed back over and I have avoided talking to him about it so far. All he knows is that the threat of war is gone and we can return home. I knew I couldn't keep him at bay much longer and I let out a heavy sigh as he approaches.

"Give it up. What happened over there?" He looms over me where I am washing up in the stream.

I stop washing and shrug my coat back on before sitting at the water's edge, refusing to meet Fergus' glare.

"If I could explain it to you, I would have by now, Ferg."

"Horseshit. What kind of an answer is that? Brandon is a bloody mess. You have to know something. We're walking away with our freedom, why? You didn't question that? You know something."

"It's Brandon's doing and honestly, I'm only just starting to understand Rovell's words now."

"Quit being so damn cryptic and who's Rovell?"

Gritting my teeth together, I glance over at Fergus, who has pulled up a piece of ground beside me. How do I explain the truth about something when I don't have any firm answers?

"Rovell is their Master, their leader. He held Brandon captive as his slave. Made some kind of deal with him for our freedom."

"What deal?"

"I don't know the specifics. All I know is, that man got so far inside Brandon's head he had him bowing to him and doing everything the man commanded. It was sickening to watch."

I pause, intent on leaving it at that, but Fergus' silence nudges me on.

"When I showed up, Rovell was happy to return Brandon to me. In fact, the bloody prick expected me. Whatever 'terms' they'd agreed upon had been met and Brandon was free to come back…Only…"

Fergus places a hand on my shoulder.

"Only what?" He urges.

"Only, you've seen him. He's not the same. Brandon begged Rovell to end his life. He was desperate not to return with me. He won't talk to me. He won't even let me go near him, let alone touch him. The look in his eyes is tearing me apart, Fergus. He's dead inside. I don't know what that man did, but my brain keeps coming up with all kinds of crazy, wild, really terrifying shit and…" I choke off the last few words, shaking my head. I can't go on.

Fergus pulls me into a bear hug and I fall heavy into his arms. Tears brim my eyes, but I force them away. Fergus is not ordinarily one for emotional displays like this and I'm already a little shocked at the embrace. The last thing he needs is for me to come completely undone. He probably wouldn't even know what to do with that. As quickly as he grabs hold of me, he soon lets me go with a ruffle of my hair.

"Fear not, brother. We'll sort Bran's head out and figure out the truth. Maybe he'll talk to me. I can try."

"Go easy on him, Fergus. I don't want him to pull further away."

* * *

Eight days into our journey home, Chase informs me he doesn't feel it is safe for Brandon to ride solo any longer. Brandon's refusal to take in more than a mouthful or two of food and even less drink has made him weak and he has threatened to fall from his saddle so many times, Chase is concerned he might end up hurt.

Seeing as Brandon will have nothing to do with me, Fergus offers to take him double on his horse. It kills me to see someone else being able to touch him and comfort him. Especially with as many times as I have been pushed away. I tell Brandon daily I will never give up on him. Whether he believes me or not, I have no idea.

In the late morning, nine days into our travel, Fergus brings his horse up beside me. Brandon has drifted off to sleep in front of him, head lulled back, softly thudding off Fergus' shoulder. His skin is pale and his dark blond hair, which has fallen across his eyes, looks darker than usual in contrast. I want to swipe it back, feel its silky smoothness in my fingers. He looks so frail and even in sleep, he looks utterly lost. My heart aches to touch him and every moment since getting him back has been torturous, having to withhold those urges in order to not upset him.

Fergus' eyes land on me and his forehead creases.

"What happened to him?"

Fergus keeps his voice low, but his question is abrupt and demanding of an answer.

"I told you. I. Don't. Know."

"Horseshit. You may not know precisely, but you have suspicions don't you?"

I glare at Fergus. *Damn right I have suspicions, in fact, I can probably guess exactly what happened to Brandon.* I remain silent and tighten my grip on the reins. Fergus isn't going to let up. I can see it in his face. The downfall at having known each other this long is that I can't hide anything from him.

"He's been abused, Alistair, and I don't mean this Rovell character beat the shit out of him or tortured him on a regular basis either." His words are blunt and his eyes never shift from mine. "He's been-"

"Don't say it!"

I look back to the dirt road ahead of me, my guts twisting inside and I grind my teeth together achingly hard.

"He cries out in his sleep, Alistair. He thrashes and tries to get away any time anyone goes near him." Fergus continues anyway. "I'm telling you, I'm not wrong."

I know he's not, but I refuse to admit it even though I saw the truth back in Rovell's tent. The vision of that man's tongue running up Brandon's neck and over his ear is so clear in my mind I could burst. The idea that someone used Brandon in such a way makes me sick and if I thought for an instant we had a fighting chance against Rovell's army, I would march across the border and wipe them out, just for revenge.

"Alistair, are you listening to me?"

"I hear you. But you don't know."

I want to remain in denial, because the truth of the matter is too much for me to bear right now.

"Quit hiding from the truth-"

"I'm not hiding, dammit! You don't think I have eyes and ears? You don't think I see what you're seeing? I'm not an idiot, but I can't… I just…" I trail off.

The truth is I *am* hiding from the truth. I'm afraid of what it could mean. I hear Rovell's taunts in my mind, that killing Brandon would have been too easy, instead I'm to watch him suffer for what Rovell did to him every day for the rest of our lives and suffer I am.

I watch Brandon's head rested on Fergus and want nothing more than to take him against my chest and hold him where he can hear my heartbeat. Tell him it beats for him alone and without him I'm lost.

Every day he seems further and further away. The sparkle I once saw in his eyes is gone and only a darkness remains. I can't even remember the last time I slept because I sit beside Brandon every night and just watch over him. Watch the nightmares when he does sleep and the faraway look in his eyes when he is awake and I wonder if he will ever come back to me or if Rovell has thoroughly destroyed my lover's soul.

A day's ride from Ludairium, I watch as Chase does everything in his power to get Brandon to eat. It's always a fight, but eventually Brandon gives in to him and takes a menial amount. What happens when he stops eating altogether? What then? He already is looking sickly and thin and I'm not sure he can afford to keep going like this.

After his usual few bites, Brandon refuses more and Chase sighs, backing down. Chase's eyes connect with mine and he shrugs. I appreciate the effort he shows with Brandon, especially since he seems to be the only person Brandon has connected with so far, though I'm hard pressed to say it is truly "connecting." More like tolerates. Why Chase, I have no idea.

Dismissing Chase with the nod of my head, I make my way over to Brandon where he sits by a newly built fire, distant as ever. Crouching down beside him, keeping a safe distance away, I do what I've been doing every day since our return; I talk to him. I never get a reply and no longer expect one, but I need him to know I will never give up.

"Honestly, that slop they're calling stew is getting worse by the day, I hardly blame you for not wanting to eat. Once we're home, I'll have something decent made and you and I can eat until we burst. Deal?"

No answer…Of course.

I let the silence grow a while, matching his empty stare into the flames.

"You know the good thing about being on the road this long? It makes sleeping in a bed when we're back feel like heaven. Since leaving Ludairium, I've done nothing more than dream about curling up beside you in our bed and having the best damn night sleep ever."

Nothing.

I stare into his profile. His eyes are half lidded and far away. His lips are slightly parted. Dark circles are vivid against his pale skin and sadness makes his normally high smiling cheeks hang. He is but a hollow shell of the man I sent north.

Where are you, B?

"Babe?" He blinks and shifts his gaze to the ground in front of me. He's listening. "I miss touching you. I wish you would let me near you. This is killing me. It's tearing me apart having to keep my hands to myself. I just want to hold you, babe, and make whatever this is better."

His forehead creases at those words, but the silence remains. I keep pushing, a little more.

"I miss making love to you. Having you wrapped all around me. Feeling our bodies joined, being one with you. You make me feel so complete. Without you, I always feel like I'm missing something."

Brandon's throat constricts as he swallows hard. He is definitely feeling my words.

"I miss kissing you the most. You have the most addictive lips." I smile thinking about it. "From the very first kiss we ever shared, way back when I didn't even know what the hell was going on inside me, I haven't been able to stop. I crave those kisses…gah…and your damn tongue, just toying with me. You own me with those moves of yours, you know that? I can never say no to you."

A gentle twitch at the corner of his lips almost looks like he could be fighting off a smile. It's the biggest connection we've made so far and I say a quick prayer to the Maker that maybe, he will find his way back.

I don't want to push too hard, so I stop there and let the silence fill the void again. When I see the other men getting ready to ride out, I stand and risk giving his shoulder a gentle squeeze.

"I'll never stop loving you, Brandon. I'll be here for you, always waiting to have those things with you again."

Chapter Thirteen

Present Day

Brandon

A stirring in the room wakes me a little after dawn. Listening intently, keeping my eyes closed, I hear what I presume is a maid servant stoking the fire. A clattering - probably dishes - are set down on the bedside table behind me. Breakfast. A soft female voice whispers something I can't hear, but it's not meant for my ears. I hear a deep throated, grumbling reply and I know he is still in the room. I shouldn't be surprised; he has barely let me out of his sight since my rescue.

I peek my eyes open and peer around my burrow of blankets without moving. The drapes are drawn closed, but the sun leaks through around the edges, creeping into the room and with it brings the promise of a new day. A new day perhaps, but wrapped in old scars, it looks just like every day before it.

I lay perfectly still. The maid servant is gone, but I can hear him shuffling and breathing behind me. He's up and pacing again; a nervous habit I've seen him do a million times before. In a previous life, I would have tried to quell his nervous energy with a kiss. Today, I just wish he would leave me alone. I wish he would go on with his life and forget I ever existed, so that I too can forget. His presence only makes everything more real and harder to get away from.

He has made a great effort to try and pull me back to this life with him and it's getting harder and harder to hold him at arm's length anymore. However, the life we shared, as beautiful as I remember it being, was based on lies and my truth is more than I wish him to know.

It was absurd to think I could form a new life for myself here in Ludairium, with him. Absurd to believe I could bury my past and not expect it to come back and laugh at me in the face. Having been hidden inside for so long, entombed for so many years, I was beginning to believe it had never existed, but that was fools thinking. My scars run deep, so deep I had been able to make them invisible to the naked eye...or so I thought, until Rovell reopened them and made them fresh again.

Today, as I lay here hiding from the morning sun and the man I once gave my life to and loved, my newly opened wounds bleed, weep, and cry out, reminding me of a time, long ago suppressed.

"B?" I feel the bed shift under his weight and I know he's sitting beside me. "B, there's food. You need to eat. Can I help you? Please."

His voice is pleading and I can hear his pain, but the hollowness inside me cannot be filled or satisfied with nourishment. It is a far greater emptiness, as though someone has raked my guts and organs clean out of my body and left me with literally nothing inside. A shell of a man, that's all I am now. I burrow deeper into my blankets in response. Wishing I could disappear.

Alistair takes hold of the blankets and gently pulls them back, trying to free me from my shelter. I tighten my grasp to keep them where they are, leaving us in a tug-o-war of power. I don't want him to see me like this and my determination wins out as he releases his grip.

I wish he would just go. I don't want to hurt him, but I'm not the man he fell in love with any longer. Why can't he see that? That man is gone. He was a lie, nothing but a fabricated, phony fairytale. One that believed in happy endings, one that hoped for a better tomorrow and dreamed of a beautiful future. I never told him who I truly was, I never explained my past. I didn't tell him about Jeremy's life. I thought if I kept it buried, if those secrets remained secrets, they could never come back and harm me. I was wrong. So. So. Wrong.

The door creaks open and the weight on the bed shifts and is gone. I let out a breath as I hear Alistair drag his feet across to the other end of the room. Muffled voices share a conversation. Low talking, too low to hear what is being said. I recognize the new voice, it's all too familiar and I sigh inwardly, knowing the drill. I've become accustomed with the routine of every day.

I can hear the new man speak encouragement to Alistair. I don't need words to hear the reassurance in his tone. Why does everyone insist on giving this man false hope? They should not have brought me back here. They should have let me go. Being here will only bring him more pain.

The door creaks again and closes. Someone has gone, but who? Footsteps approach the bed. They are not burdened with the same sadness and defeat as before so I assume they are not those of Alistair, which means Chase has convinced him to take a walk. Surprisingly, Chase has been the only man to have any ability to control Alistair since we returned to Edovia. Alistair hangs on his every word and deep down, the old me wants to come to the surface and smile at the irony.

Chase nears the bed on the side closest to where I lay and pulls back the covers forcefully. I don't resist. This man has seen my demons and I can't hide from him like I can anyone else.

"You're eating, like it or not." Chase shadows the sun leaking around the drapes with his body and glares down at me.

He places his hands on my shoulders and flips me over to my back. For a man significantly smaller than me, I'm amazed at his ability to manipulate me. Sprawled on my back, he props my head up with a rolled up blanket under my head and sits beside me. With a hand under my chin, he forces my face to look at his, tilting my head side to side as he examines me. The green of his eyes is darker than usual and they shift back and forth between my eyes. A finger gently pulls the skin down under each eye, one at a time as he studies them. He frowns. His eyebrows knit together as he inhales deeply.

"You're losing weight and you're white as a ghost." When he releases my chin, I turn my face away.

Chase has been telling me the same thing since I crossed back over into Edovia. On our travels south, back to Ludairium, he forced as much food into me as I would take until I fought him off. The closer we got to home, the more reluctant I became.

Food does nothing more than accentuate the feeling of nausea in my belly. I no longer feel hunger and I no longer care if I live or die. People should respect my decision and quit acting like they know what's best for me. I know what's best for me, and for everyone around me. I can't take anymore and I want to curl up in my hovel of blankets and let the Maker take me home. I'm not Brandon Leeson, Brandon Leeson's life was nothing but a lie. This is not my life anymore and I'm so tired. I just want to break free.

Chase rises and moves around the bed to the night table on the other side where the maid servant has placed my meal. I close my eyes and try to envision my body rising to the heavens. If I could die from shear willpower, I would be gone by now. Soon. Life can only be sustained so long as a person is willing to be a part of it, right? Once you give up, it is only a matter of time. *I'm ready. Please let me go.*

"You can try to hide all you want, but it's not going to work with me and you know it, so give it up."

I open my eyes and see Chase standing over me stirring the contents of the bowl, glaring at me.

"Better. Thank you." He says as he kneels down on the bed beside me and presses the spoon to my lips. I shift my eyes from Chase's down to the beige mush being pressed to my mouth.

"Open." Chase demands.

I curl my nose and don't immediately obey. The spoon pushes harder against my mouth and I can taste the sweetness of the honey that has been mixed in with the oat gruel on my lips.

"I swear to the Maker himself, I will sit here all day if I have to. Open your damn mouth and eat, Brandon. Quit being so damn stubborn. This stuff only gets worse as it cools."

Reluctantly, I crack my lips open a slit and allow Chase to shove as much of the spoonful into my mouth as he can. I fight him for another four bites then bat the spoon away and roll over on my side again, pulling the blankets to cover me to my neck.

"That's hardly enough."

I ignore him. Chase doesn't persist anymore and I hear him set the bowl back on the tray. He moves to the window and pulls the drapes aside letting in the morning sun. I watch him as he stares out across the field and into the forest beyond. He tucks a few strands of chestnut brown hair back behind his ear that have fallen from the tie binding it behind his head. He turns from the window after a few moments and comes back around to sit on the bed beside me. Taking my hand in his he strokes his fingers gently over the surface as worry crosses his face.

"You need to talk about it, because it's eating you alive. I can't watch you destroy yourself, Brandon."

I gaze past Chase to the window and the blue sky beyond. There is a scattering of gray clouds floating along with a gentle breeze. Spring has barely graced Edovia and the remaining evidence of winter can be found in the trace bits of snow and ice remaining on the bare tree branches.

"Brandon." His voice is barely past a whisper. "Have you ever told Alistair what you told me?"

My eyes shoot back to his and my heart jumps in my chest, suddenly pounding so fast it hurts against my ribcage.

"I'll take that as a no." He says.

I pull myself to a sit and take Chase's arms tight in my grasp, digging my fingers into him as fear rips through me.

"You can't tell him." My voice is raspy and cracks from not having been used in so long.

Chase squirms under my hold and he reaches up to try and peel my hands off him. It only encourages me to hold him tighter.

"Brandon, you're hurting me."

I look to where I'm holding him and release my grip. I hadn't meant to hurt him. I'm trembling and Chase takes my hands in his before I can pull them away.

"Bloody hell, Brandon. You're shaking."

"Please don't tell him, he can't know."

Chase takes me in his arms and holds me tight, stroking my hair and rocking me against his body.

"Did Rovell do what I think he did, Brandon?"

Squeezing my eyes shut tight I try to put myself somewhere else. A lake. Fish. Birds. When the memories I've tried to block filter into my head regardless, I tighten my grip around Chase. I can't stop shaking. Can't stop gasping in each breath as though my lungs are thirsty for air and I can't fulfil their need. When I don't answer, he tries another approach.

"Can you tell me what happened?"

More panting breaths. What happened? The world is cruel, that's what happened. Everything I worked so hard to build and everything I tried so hard to forget were thrown back in my face in an instant and I had to make a choice. Rovell made me choose. He reduced me to the scared little boy I had been growing up, stripped me of everything I had built. He made me choose damn it, and I chose to save our realm despite all consequences to myself. I chose to save tens of thousands for the cost of my soul. I chose to rip off the tourniquet holding me together and let my old wounds bleed freely. Let my haunting past reclaim me. That is what happened.

Chase pulls me back from his chest and looks deep into my eyes, searching for answers. His hand grazes up and down my arm, trying for comfort, trying to draw me out.

"Brandon. You have to let it out."

My vision blurs and his face distorts with my flood of tears. My chin quivers as he brushes them away.

"I made a choice." My voice chokes up and I'm not even sure the words are clear enough to be heard. "I saved our realm."

Chapter Fourteen

Alistair

With my teeth, I rip the dangling nail from my thumb, tearing with it a piece of the tender flesh from underneath. I curse under my breath as blood rises to the surface of my now raw nub while I stick it in my mouth to soothe the sting rising from the torn skin and taste the tang of copper at the back of my throat. I need to stop abusing my damn fingers. I have chewed every one of them bloody with the stress of the past winter and they ache now from the abuse.

The door to my bed chambers remains closed and I spin again on my feet, retracing the short width of the hallway in my endless pace as I wait. I stare at the ground, anticipating there will soon be a worn spot where my boots have been treading for the last half of the morning.

Chase has yet to emerge and the longer he's in there, the more restless I'm becoming. There was a time when Chase being alone in a room with Brandon would have sent me into an all-out rage of worry and jealousy, but those days are behind me. Brandon's old lover no longer sets the hair on my arms to rise. We have found a peace with each other and now I'm putting all my hope in the man and his ability to get some answers about what happened across the border and help soothe Brandon out of his state.

When the door to my bed chambers finally opens, my head flies up to see Chase, tray of food balanced on his hip, as he sets the door closed again in his wake.

"Anything?" I can't hide the desperation from my voice. There are so many questions I want answers to and Brandon is the only one who can give them.

"He ate about five bites. It's more than he had last night, but his eyes are sunk in and his skin is gray. It's not enough, and he needs to drink too and I can't convince him to take more than a mouthful or two. This isn't enough to sustain him. He's weaker every day."

I nod my head as he speaks and swallow the bile back down my throat. It's been the same story since we crossed back over and I don't know what to do about it. Brandon has become downright stubborn.

Chase places the food tray on the ground outside the door for the maid servant to pick up later and puts his hands on his hips, shaking his head.

"He spoke to me. Only a few words, but it's a huge start."

"What? He did? What did he say?" Aside from crying out in his sleep, Brandon hasn't said much of anything since we were in Rovell's tent, over a fortnight ago.

"I asked him what happened."

"Did he tell you? Maker, please say he told you."

"Not precisely. He says he made a choice and he chose to save our realm."

I blink at Chase and search his face for more. There is no more. Chase shrugs his shoulders.

"That's it. I tried to have him explain what choice he needed to make, but he pulled away and wouldn't engage anymore."

"So he was given some sort of ultimatum do you think?"

"Something like that."

"What the bloody hell does that mean? What choice? What happened to him?"

Chase has no answers and just stares at me with sympathetic eyes. It's the same damn look everyone keeps giving me. Everyone knows what happened to him, including me, only I can't seem to admit it out loud. By staying silent, not giving the truth a voice, maybe it won't be real.

"Why won't he talk to me? He won't even look at me and every time I try to touch him…" I bite back the fear from my voice, "he withdraws from me. He can't stand my touch."

Chase looks worn out. He tucks a few loose strands of hair behind his ear and grimaces as he meets my gaze.

"Alistair… I have theories and so do you. I think we need to accept the truth and quit denying it."

I blink back the tears pooling in my eyes. "He was raped wasn't he?" My voice is barely a whisper as I voice my worst fear. Hearing myself say it turns my legs to jelly and I lean hard on the wall, sliding down to sit. My hands shake violently as I keep my eyes trained on Chase.

Chase purses his lips and nods. "I think that's part of it. There are no signs that I saw of him being restrained. If he was bound, he didn't struggle. There were no marks on his wrists or ankles. I examined him as much as he would allow and I saw nothing to tell me for sure."

"He didn't fight it. He gave up. Chase, when I went to rescue him and Rovell set us free, he begged the man to end his life. He didn't want to come back with me. I don't understand."

No amount of blinking is holding back all the tears, and a few persistent ones fall down my cheek uninvited and I swipe them away quickly, hoping Chase doesn't see me falling apart.

Chase comes up in front of me and squats down taking my trembling hands in his. His touch sends me over the edge as lack of sleep and stress take me over and violent sobs rack my body. Chase, of all people, wraps his arms around me and just holds me as I lose all control. I hate myself with every fiber of my being for showing weakness. I'm supposed to be the strong one right now, but I can hardly hold myself up anymore.

"Don't give up on him, Alistair. He needs you. He just doesn't know it."

"I would never give up on him. That man owns half my soul and I can't live without him. I hate what Rovell did to him."

As Chase holds me, I unleash all the pent up feelings I've been holding on to all winter. What happens now? What if I never get my Brandon back?

"Alistair. What has Brandon shared with you about his past?"

Confused by the question, I lift my head from Chase's shoulder, wipe my face of the evidence of my meltdown and look at him, seeing concern etched in the crinkles of his eyes.

"What do you mean?"

"About his growing up. What has he shared with you?"

I shake my head, still not following what Chase is saying. "He grew up in Creston. After his mother abandoned him, the minister raised him until he was sixteen and the man died. Why?"

"How about before that. Before his mother abandoned him? When he lived with his parents."

An eerie shiver crawls up the back of my neck. Brandon has been very protective about that part of his past, he has told me little and I've never pushed the issue. I always figured he'd share when he was ready.

I shake my head. "He's never told me anything about that far back. I only know he went by another name then and that he changed it after his mother abandoned him. He said he needed to forget his past, all of it. He wanted to build himself a different life. A better one."

"Jeremy Weston." Chase says, matter of fact.

"That's it, yeah."

Chase lowers his head, averting his eyes and goes quiet.

"You know something." I can see it in his face and body language.

Chase lets out a deep sigh and meets my eyes again. He looks as though he is considering something and there is a long pause before he continues.

"We should probably talk. There is something you should know and Brandon will hate me for telling you, but I think in light of everything that is going on, it's important."

My heart hammers inside my chest as I let Chase help me off the floor.

"Should I have someone sit with him? Do you think he'll be okay alone?"

I haven't left Brandon unattended for any reason, especially since he fought me to get at the dagger I didn't have and tried to run once we hit camp. I'm not sure I trust him to be alone.

"He seemed like he was going to sleep when I left. He'll be fine."

Chase gives my hand a squeeze.

"Okay. How about we go to my solar. It's just down the hall."

"You might want to make sure you have some whiskey on hand." Chase says as an afterthought, giving me a sad smirk.

"That bad?"

He nods and drops my hand before heading down the hall.

"I'll meet you there." He says.

* * *

After I secure myself a new, full jug of whiskey, I head to my solar. My mind is swimming and my heart hasn't settled in my chest. Deep inside I know whatever it is Chase is about to share with me is bad. If he knows something about Brandon's past, it is because Brandon has shared something with him that he has never shared with me. The thought alone bothers me. Why would Brandon not trust me enough to share his past with me when he has already shared whatever it is with Chase?

That stupid twinge of jealousy tickles my insides and I push it away. Besides, I wonder if I'd be better off not knowing. If it's as bad as I think it will be, it will only break my heart even more.

A million thoughts fly through my head, each one more desperate and horrifying than the last and I can't still my mind. Entering the solar, I see Chase seated at a chair he has pulled up to my desk. He glances briefly over his shoulder and goes back to studying his hands in his lap.

I move across the room, grabbing a pair of glasses as I pass the bar table and settle into the chair across from him. Without asking, I pour two glasses of whiskey and slide one across to him. He eyes it and I see him wince.

"Not a fan I take it."

"Not really, but I may need it after this."

Chase may not be a whiskey lover, but I am and right now I need a good steadying glass to calm my erratic nerves before I throw up. Downing my first drink without pause, I refill it while studying Chase's downcast eyes. The man looks distraught and his tension is only making mine worse.

"Talk, Chase. Don't sit on whatever the hell you know, you're killing me."

Chase closes his eyes and inhales an audible breath before raising his head. He presses his lips together, setting his jaw.

"He's told you nothing of his life when he lived with his parents?" Chase asks me again.

"No, I've known there was something he was hiding, but I never pushed him to tell me. I always figured he would in time."

"He wouldn't have. I assure you. He would take it to the grave, I guarantee it."

"But you know. He told you."

"He didn't want to and I forced it out of him one night. Got him right, slobbering drunk and pushed the issue. I'm not proud of myself and I've regretted it every day since. He didn't talk to me for a long time after that, and to this day, he's never forgiven me for it. He hates that I know."

"Brandon is a forgiving person, he avoids conflict and anger at all cost. He doesn't hate anyone."

"Exactly. What does that say about what I'm going to tell you right now?"

I keep my eyes trained on Chase, the crawling sensation is back and it is working its way over my entire body now, making my fine hairs stand on end.

"What happened?"

Chase meets my eyes and I can see pain and regret in them. He looks through me into the past when he speaks, to a time years ago when he broke my man's trust and forced something from him he never wanted to share.

"Like me, you probably assume you know a little of what he went through at home. I always assumed he was beaten regularly and coming from a violent home made him withdraw from his past…"

"It's more than that isn't it? I've always had an inkling it was more."

Chase refocuses on me and nods, "You're right."

"Go on."

"He actually was rarely beaten, that would have required his parents acknowledging his existence. He was locked away in his room and forgotten about. Sometimes he'd go days without food or drink, until he'd sneak out a window and steal from the neighbors in order to keep himself alive. He never ran away because he longed for his parents' love and tried endlessly to please them and find some way to not have them not hate him so much. They lived beyond the edge of poverty, his father never had steady work and sometimes they couldn't pay their rents. They didn't want a child and the extra expense at having one only made his life worse. They resented him and his existence. Over time it got more and more difficult for his father to get work. He was a raging alcoholic and no one would hire him anymore. His parents became desperate to keep themselves fed, never mind Brandon. One day, after having been locked away for days on end, his father unbarred the door to his room and brought in a well-groomed man, clearly a man of wealth. Brandon was eight years old. His father talked sweetly to Brandon in a way he'd never spoken to him before and Brandon says he remembers being confused-"

"Chase. Stop."

My chest aches from the pounding it is taking from my poor heart and my gut is roiling. I'm already one step ahead of him and I'm not sure I can hear him go on. I want to be wrong, but if I'm right, I can't hear the story like this, I might break. I down my third glass of whiskey and pour another, not pausing before draining it as well.

"Just say it straight. I can't hear a play by play, no matter how he told it to you, I just…I can't. What happened?"

Chase nods and looks to his hands again, fidgeting, his mouth working around words he can hardly say. "His parents started selling his body for money. Wealthy men paid a hefty sum to have sex with Brandon."

My world waivers in front of me at Chase's words. All the whiskey I've drank roils in my gut and I can feel it working its way back up my throat. I fly out of my seat, and yank the doors open to my terrace where I empty my stomach of its contents. A cold sweat covers my body and I fall to my knees, holding the terrace wall to steady myself as I try to take in deep breaths.

It's worse than I feared. My Brandon has truly walked the road to hell and has carried this secret with him his entire life. He never told me. Part of me is so hurt that he never felt he could trust me enough to let me know. The other part of me wants to unhear what was just said.

A hand on my shoulder startles me from my thoughts and I fight to regain my ground and stand up on shaky legs. Chase steadies my arm and doesn't let go when I turn to him.

"I reacted pretty much the same way. I'm sorry I had to be the one to tell you this."

I lean hard on the stone wall surrounding the terrace and let the cold breeze blow across my face and skin. Chase leans beside me and tilts his head to look up to the sky. I follow his gaze and watch the heavy, gray clouds above. A late winter storm is moving in and our clear, promising morning is all but gone. So much for our hopes of spring.

"Alistair, I'm telling you this for a reason, not to break your heart. I know what this knowledge is doing to you right now, because I know what it did to me when I found out. When Brandon told me about what he went through, he was so far gone with drink, but it didn't stop the impact that telling me had on him. He withdrew. He wouldn't see me or let me anywhere near him for a long time. Jefferson became concerned and called a doctor in because Brandon stopped helping in the stables and stayed curled up in a blanket hiding from the world. He became vacant and…well…lost."

"Like what he's doing now."

"Yeah."

"Is that why you think he was…raped?" I hate the word. I hate hearing myself say it.

"Something sent him back there, to that place in his mind where he has to pull away and fight to find his way back, something caused it. I think it's his way of protecting himself from the world."

"If he was used that way again…" I say, trailing off.

"He'd be in rough shape."

"Like he is."

"It just makes sense in my mind." Chase says.

I let out a defeated breath. "I need to make him talk to me. I need to know what really happened and stop all this guessing horseshit. I can't take it. He has to know I'd accept him regardless. I don't fault him."

"Tread carefully, Alistair. And, what I told you, it would be best you try to get it out of him yourself. Knowing I broke his confidence will only make him feel more ashamed I think."

I nod and bring my eyes back to Chase beside me. A year has done me and him a lot of good. The hostility between us is gone and instead I feel like I've gained an important friend. I owe this man so much for what he's taken on this past winter. The least I can do is apologize.

"I'm sorry I've been such an ass to you all this time. You're really a decent person and maybe I can kind of understand what Brandon may have seen in you all those years ago."

Chase raises his eyebrow and sideways glances at me.

"Careful, Alistair Ellesmere, that nearly sounded like a compliment."

Offering a sad smirk - the weight of our previous discussion making it hard to put out anymore - I nudge his shoulder with mine. "Yeah, it was and it may be the only one I ever give you so take it."

We stare at each other for a while longer before I push off the wall and head back inside.

"I'm going to go see how he's doing. Try and get him to talk to me."

"I'll come by later, if he hasn't eaten more then I'll force it down his stubborn ass throat. If I don't get home to Aaron soon he's gonna worry something more is wrong. He's feeling kind of neglected lately."

Turning back to Chase I pause and meet his eyes.

"Thank you, Chase. Sincerely. I know I've already pulled you two apart all winter and I really appreciate your helping Brandon out. I hope Aaron can understand."

"He does. He worries for Brandon too. Everyone is worried about him, Alistair. Rumors are circulating. The people don't know what to think."

"I should probably try to explain some if this. I just don't know what to tell them."

"In time. Rumors are just that, rumors. Brandon is what's important right now. The people will wait. Take care of him."

"Thanks, Chase."

Chapter Fifteen

Brandon

I have to get away from here.

It's the first moment I have been left alone since returning to Edovia and it may be my only chance for escape.

When Chase walked out, I fully expected Alistair to return right away, like he always does. The man has not left my side for any reason except when Chase asks him to so he can shove food into me or try to provoke conversation for which I'll have no part of.

I lay waiting for his return, but time passes and he doesn't come back. At first I think I may have missed him slipping silently into the room and chance a discreet look around, but he's not here. My mind races at the thought of an opportunity to break away. I ignore my treacherous heart, begging me not to do this. I have to break free. It is best for everyone that I be gone and I may never get another opportunity.

I sit up in bed and steady my feet on the floor. Dark spots swim across my vision and I momentarily feel as though I'm going to faint. I close my eyes and wait for it to pass. I'm weak, extremely weak, and need to move cautiously.

My heart hammers at the thought that Alistair could return at any moment and catch me in the act of leaving. I know the man will be utterly devastated when he finds out I'm gone, but he will recover…in time. Staying, fighting back, and fitting back into my fabricated lie of a life wouldn't be fair to him. I love him too much to hurt him anymore, and the only thing he loves about me, is my lie. He could never love the man I truly am. No one could. Why am I the only person who can see this? Jeremy was never meant to be loved.

I stand, putting weight on my trembling legs and hold still for a moment while I gather the strength to take a few steps. I can hear the blood pounding in my ears and my vision swims again before clearing almost right away. *This is going to be harder than I thought.*

Once in motion, I try to move fast. I grab a change of clothes from my chest in the corner and shove them in a small satchel. I make quick work of tugging on my boots, leaving them unbuckled, while I snag Alistair's riding coat off the back of the chair. I can't see mine and refuse to waste any more time looking for it.

I throw the coat over my thin shirt. It's a little big on me, Alistair being broader in the shoulders and thicker with muscle across the chest has always made his clothes hang off me a bit uncannily, despite the fact that he has always liked me wearing his clothes.

The scent of Alistair lingering on the jacket nearly knocks me to my knees. I haven't allowed him to get close enough to be wrapped up in his intoxicating essence and I tremble uncontrollably as I hold the collar to my nose and inhale deeply. Taking this coat is going to be sweet torture.

At the door, I put my ear to the wood and listen for any signs that someone might be on the other side, or coming down the hall. I hear nothing. Resting my hand on the cool handle, I try to calm the jitters shaking through my body. I pull the door open enough to get my body through and slide out doing a scan of the hallway. It's clear.

I move quickly to the servant's alcove further down the hall and duck inside, intent on taking the back way out of the castle. Taking the stairs two at a time, I try hard not to stumble. My head feels light and my movements all feel as though they are happening in slow motion. Keeping my hand on the wall for balance, I manage to get to the bottom without incident.

I should have accepted more food from Chase, I'm not sure I have the strength to get far enough away. In retrospect, I never thought I'd get away at all, I assumed to just let myself slowly die of my own free will from sheer lack of desire to live anymore. With an escape available, I'm cursing my previous choices; wishing I had even an ounce of capacity to go on so I can get as far away as possible. At this rate, I'll be lucky if I manage to get out of the castle before succumbing to weakness. That's all I need; Alistair to find me passed out on the floor somewhere.

At the bottom of the stairs, I lean a moment to let my head clear and get my bearings. I'm dizzy and my brain is having trouble keeping up with my body.

Having pulled open a back door to the castle, I head into the gardens. Weaving through the dormant passages of vegetation, I make my way to the stone wall surrounding the training field. Pulling myself over the wall proves to be a challenge and shows just how frail I have become.

This ordinarily easy task, that I have done hundreds of times, is almost impossible now. I lose my grip and slide, crashing bodily into the ground more than once before finally succeeding in making it over. Once on the other side, I scurry as quickly as my legs will carry me to get to the southeast end of the field where another wall holds the forest at bay.

I feel exposed in the open field and check over my shoulder obsessively, expecting someone to be on my heels at any moment, ready to drag me back to the castle. Not for the first time, I say a grateful prayer that Alistair keeps minimal guards on duty.

After scaling the second wall - with no more ease than the first - and falling to the ground on the other side - landing on my ass when my legs give out - I know I can't go much farther. My body is already battered and fresh bruises are forming where my clumsiness and inability to function properly has played against me. I fight to keep going, knowing I can't stay here. Knowing I must keep pushing forward.

I rise to my feet again and continue to move along, away from the castle, away from everything that was once my life. My world is spinning around me, the black spots fade back into my vision and I stumble over my own feet repeatedly as I try to make my way through the forest. The tangle of branches and undergrowth is too much to process and my legs won't respond properly when my brain says to lift them higher.

I fall again, jarring my left arm, sending a stabbing pain straight to my shoulder, aggravating an old injury. I suck in a sharp breath and cradle my arm for a moment while it passes.

My legs shake underneath me as I pull to stand again, but I wobble and struggle to stay on my feet. Leaning hard against a tree while I catch my breath, I consider my options. I'm too weak. There is no way I'll make it anywhere with the state I'm in. I push off the tree and continue along, slowing my pace to a brisk walk and decide to head straight for the cottage in the woods. My old home and sanctuary.

Since moving into the castle a year ago, it sits empty. Alistair and I have used it frequently to sneak off and have some true privacy together when the need arises. With him being King, it was required more times than not. Privacy is nearly a redundant word in Alistair's world and unless we made it for ourselves, it didn't happen.

It's a terrible hiding place and I know it, but I need to get my feet beneath me and find something to eat if I'm going to be strong enough to get away. At this rate, I'll be lucky if they don't find me around the next bend curled up in a little ball.

Ordinarily, Alistair and I would keep a stash of food and drink at the cottage for our little getaways, but seeing as we haven't been here all winter it's doubtful there will be anything on hand. All I can do is hope. I need to eat, get some strength back, and pack a few things before I can make it out on my own. I have no direction, no destination, and no plan. I just know I can't stay here.

At the cottage, I let myself in and make quick work of rummaging through the pantry, hoping to find something to eat. I become more frantic as I realize there is nothing here. All I find is a half jug of ale and a fuzzy, round ball of green that I assume may have once been a heel of bread. *Disgusting.*

I pull the stopper off the jug and sniff its contents before lifting it to my mouth and draining a few deep swallows. The near freezing liquid can be felt as it travels all the way down my throat into my belly and sends a shiver threw my body. It tastes okay and my stomach rewards me with an audible groan. It's the first time I have felt anything close to hunger in ages.

Drinking a little more, I bring the jug with me into my old bed chambers where I place it on the floor and collapse onto the pile of blankets left strewn over the pallet. My body is so weak and tired, I need to rest some and figure out what I'm going to do. I can't stay long. He'll find me here. I know he will. I bury my face into the rumpled covers and close my eyes remembering the last time I was here in this room, on this bed.

Alistair and I had been working excruciating long days, organizing our journey north and planning everything for the negotiations with the Outsiders. Meeting after meeting with the council and even after retiring for the night, we were never left alone. The constant interruption and intrusion into our privacy was too much to take, so we came here to get away for a night.

It was two nights before I left with the party and rode north. We didn't sleep a wink. We had made love all night, unable to keep our hands off of each other. Unable to stop for anything, not even a little sleep. That's how it is with us or rather, how it was. Our appetites for each other were insatiable, ones that could never be quenched. The way Alistair always knew exactly what I needed and how I could read him just as easily, made us able to communicate without ever saying a thing. We let our bodies do the talking more times than not and that is exactly how that last night here at the cabin had been.

I feel hollow at the memory. My stomach twists with the knowledge that I will never know those moments together with him again, but I remind myself it was all a lie. That was Brandon's life, not Jeremy's. No one can love Jeremy. But, against my will, I miss him.

I have never known love like I did with Alistair. I have never had anyone fight so hard for me, for us, as that man did to give us our freedom last winter. I wonder if the ache in my heart will ever subside. If my body will ever accept the life I will now live without him. The emptiness I feel, knowing I must leave, knowing I'm giving up the only person who has ever made me feel alive, sends my body into an uncontrollable release. I can't stop it or hold it in. The longing and loss of all that I once had surfaces and I can't hold it back any longer.

Tears stream down my face without mercy and I cry. My body gives up the fight and my soul pours out in retched, painful sobs. Violently I cry, soaking the blankets beneath me and making my body convulse and ache as the fight drains from me. I've never felt so lost and so alone. So undeserving of life.

Chapter Sixteen

Alistair

  I stand watching the anguish roll off of him in waves as he pours tears into the blankets underneath him. He's been crying uncontrollably since I arrived before dusk. He doesn't know I'm here and I have done nothing more than stand back and watch him as my heart shatters into a million pieces. I fear his rejection, but want nothing more than to take away his hurt, a hurt I now understand runs far deeper than I ever could have guessed.

  When I found him missing, I panicked. I searched the room, the surrounding rooms, and was tearing down the castle halls to the front exit when clarity hit me and I knew without a shadow of a doubt where I'd find him. I was right. Subconsciously, I wonder if he wanted to be found.

  Brandon always laughed at how in tune to each other we were. It only made sense that I would find him here. The cottage has always been our escape from the world and as much as I know he is running from me, it's the one place where I know he feels safe.

  I never told him how I saw the sense of security the cottage gave him, how every time his mind and life overwhelmed him, he suggested a night here. I kept that information to myself. It's how I knew where he was at. The man has always held himself behind a very impenetrable wall, but over time, I've learned to see when he was struggling to keep it in place.

  I've been watching Brandon and deciding the best course of action to take. He has spent far more than a moons turn pushing me away, and now, thanks to Chase, I may have figured out why. I've decided I need to be aggressive in my approach, no more waiting for him to come around. He needs to face his demons and me in the process. I have just been trying to strum up the nerve to do what needs to be done.

Taking a deep breath, I approach him from behind and don't hesitate when I peel him off the bed and fold him into my arms. He startles at my presence and looks back at me, instantly trying to rip himself free from my touch. I refuse to allow it this time and grip my hands tight around his wrists taking him into a backwards hug, curling my arms around him, holding him tight to my body. He resists for only a few more tries before giving in and slumping into my hold, sobbing with more heartbreaking tears than I can take. I hold him against my body and kiss his cheek and neck, his wet tears leaving salty streaks down his face.

"Shhh, babe. I got you."

I don't let go. I continue with gentle words and touches as waves of grief pour out of him. Only now do I understand just how truly broken this man must be feeling and the fact that all I can do is hold him doesn't feel like enough. I hold him until his crying eases somewhat and he leans his head back onto my shoulder, exhaustion weighing his body heavy against me.

"You have to let me go." He says between hiccupped gulps of air.

"You know I can't do that. I love you too much, Brandon. I'll never let you go, babe. Never."

"But it's all a lie. Everything about me is a bloody lie. You don't even know who I truly am. All you love is who you think I am."

"Then tell me, Brandon. Stop shutting me out. I swear to you on my father's grave I will love you still, even when I know the truth."

Releasing my hold, I bring myself around to sit in front of him and bring his face up to look me in the eyes. He is so sad and lost, his eyes swollen from crying out a lifetime of pain, but seeing them makes my heart swell and the love I have for him consumes me. The desire to take his pain from him runs deep and I wish, for even an instant, I could give him some relief.

"Brandon," I plea, "You own my heart and my soul. It's scary how much power you hold over me. No matter what has happened in your past and no matter what the future holds, I love you and I will be by your side. Nothing will ever change that. Please talk to me, babe. Lean on me. Let me take some of that hurt on my shoulders for you and let me be your strength."

Brandon's eyes are unfocused as he stares off to a distant corner of the room. I can't be sure if he is listening or even considering what I'm saying, for all I know he is shutting down again and blocking me out.

I draw him into my arms and he comes willingly, resting his head on my chest where I hold him, stroking his hair and kissing his head. The remnants of his breakdown evident as his body sucks in deep gulps of air every so often. I don't let go, even long after his breathing has settled back to normal and the moon reaches high in the sky, moving past my view in the window.

The comfort I feel at having him back in my arms brings on a sense of relief in itself and exhaustion takes its hold. My eyes close and I can feel sleep trying to pull me down, but I don't let go of him. I'm nodding off when I hear Brandon's soft voice talking into my chest. It is nothing more than a whisper across the dark room, but I'm wide awake again. Listening.

"My parents sold my body for money. I was raped so many times as a child I can't even remember how many. So many times, I quit fighting them off and just gave in and let them have what they wanted, because it was easier."

I set my jaw as I listen, fearing his every word, knowing how hard this must be to speak out loud. My arms squeeze him tighter as he speaks and I fight back my own tears, intent on staying strong for him. Thank the Maker Chase already told me, I would never have made it through his confession otherwise.

"The day my mother sent me away, I remember hearing a man in our house. I figured it was just another, coming to take what he wanted from me, but it wasn't. I didn't hear the conversation, but it was heated and I heard my name being thrown around. After the man left, my parents argued and next I knew I was being dragged out of town…" he trails off, "you know the rest. I think they got caught. I think that man was issuing a warning and their only solution was to dispose of me. They never loved me."

I lace my fingers through his hair and run a hand up and down his back. He hasn't pulled away and he's talking to me, all good signs.

After a while Brandon lifts his face to me and pulls out of my arms. I want to fight to keep him there, but I know he's taken big steps already and I hate to push too hard. He stands and starts pacing. I follow him with my eyes. He stares at the ground as he walks. I don't even have the right words to say to him. What do you say to a revelation like that? Nothing.

Stopping mid pace, Brandon raises his gaze to meet mine. The worry etched in his forehead and the sadness drooping his features pains me.

"I have to leave, Alistair. I can't be with you anymore."

My heart picks up in my chest and the air around me becomes thick.

"Brandon." I rise from the bed and approach him only to be stopped by his extended hand keeping me at bay.

"No, don't try to stop me. You know now and that's why I must go."

"You're leaving because you think I wouldn't want you after knowing the truth? Brandon, you've never lied to me. I always knew there was something in your past that troubled you and I never pushed you to know what it was. I always assumed in time you might share with me. You've never made me believe different. I can't imagine for a second what that has done to you and how you even managed to pick yourself up and move forward after something so horrible, but I wouldn't for an instant hold it against you."

"It's more than that."

"Then what? Why are you leaving?"

His head drops and he stares at the floor again. He doesn't respond right away. He walks to the window and stands looking outside where a thick snow has begun to fall and cover the trees and ground.

"Rovell."

The chill that crawls over my skin makes me inadvertently shudder. I cautiously approach Brandon and stand behind him at the window, close enough his sweet essence hits my nose, but not close enough to touch him.

"What happened over there, B?"

He watches the snow fall silently and doesn't speak. I reach a hand up and place it on the small of his back to encourage him to continue. He stiffens at my touch, but doesn't step away.

"I was supposed to die over there. I wasn't supposed to come back."

"Did he rape you?" I have to know. I don't want to know, but everything screaming inside me has to have an answer.

"No…" He takes a breath as though he wants to say more, but he goes silent again.

Relief floods through me at his answer, but somehow I know it to be momentary and that there is far more to this then he's yet said. I rub my hand across his back, watching his blank stare out the window. His eyes pool again with tears.

"If I stay here he wins. If I stay, you will look at me every day and know what that man did and how he broke me…and ruined us, and that is exactly what he wanted. To hurt you and remind you of the cost of your freedom so you will never forget."

I risk stepping closer and wrap my arms around him. The tears trail down his face at my embrace and I turn him in my arms to cup his cheeks and wipe them away.

"What did he do to you, Brandon?"

"As a child, when the men came to take what they wanted from me, I learned that fighting them off only made it worse. If you gave them what they wanted, it was over faster. I just learned to shut down."

"Rovell?"

"It was the cost of our freedom. I agreed to become his servos and to do all jobs pertaining to that position. He wanted all of me and if I didn't go to him willingly, he swore to wipe us out and seeing the fraction of the armies he had with him, I knew he could. We didn't stand a chance. I didn't see his deeper plan until it was too late. I should have known."

"He raped you."

"He didn't, it was only a deal if I went willingly… so I did. I just shut down and gave him what he wanted like when I was a child. I didn't fight. I assumed when he tired of me, he planned to kill me and I welcomed the thought. All servos were killed when a replacement was found. My duties to him should have been limited. I didn't think I was ever coming back to you at that point. I never expected to be released. I didn't see his bigger plan and I hate myself for being so stupid, so blind to it."

The tears are flowing relentlessly now and I can't wipe them all away and instead let them fall as I look into his eyes, now a darker, angrier gray than I have ever seen before. His bottom lip is raw where he has chewed it mercilessly. The emptiness inside him scares me. He's so withdrawn I fear I may never pull him back.

"Brandon, this isn't your fault. None of it."

"You have to let me go, Alistair. I can't stay here. I can't live with this shame. Don't you see? He wins if I stay. You will never look at me the same again. Every time you see me, you will see what he has done. I've gone willingly to the bed of another man and…"

"You saved our world, Brandon. If you leave me, in my eyes, then Rovell has truly won, because you let him ruin us as well. We are stronger than this, than him. I don't blame you for what you felt you had to do."

"He should have killed me. He was supposed to kill me."

Swiping away more tears, I caress his cheeks and move so Brandon has to look me in the eyes.

"I'm glad he didn't. When I came to find you, it was my greatest fear. Nothing else mattered except that you were alive. I didn't even care for my own safety, only yours. Brandon, I couldn't breathe a full breath without knowing you were okay. You've changed my life, you brought me hope when I had none left. We are made for each other and you know that. Don't leave, don't give Rovell that power."

"Why would you want me? I've willingly betrayed our relationship. I've been dishonest about my past. The life I was trying to live was a sad attempt at covering up a seriously damaged person, Alistair."

"First of all, you did what you did for every person in Edovia. What kind of King or man would I be to punish you for the choice you made? You saved our world. You were not dishonest about your past, we've been over this. You shelter yourself from it, and Maker help me, I can see why. I can't imagine walking a day in your place. You had every right to try to make yourself a better life and dammit, I want to be there and help you do it. You deserve it. Do you have any idea the love I have for you?"

Brandon tries to pull from my grasp, his tears rolling unstopped down his face into my hands. "No one can love me, Alistair. No one."

"Do not pull away from me, Brandon. Listen to me."

"You don't want me anymore. I'm damaged, broken, a nobody. I'm nothing. I never was. I've never been anything but a discarded, unwanted child."

"You're wrong. You're everything...my everything, Brandon." I stare into his beautiful face and know without a doubt that it's the truth. "You know what?"

I take both his hands and pull him away from the window and take him back to the bed, sitting him down. I kneel before him, nestling myself between his legs and stare up into his defeated face, taking his cheeks back into my hands.

"Listen to me, babe. Since you've come into my life, everything has changed. Everything is better. Things that would drive me crazy before and get under my skin don't, because I know I have you and none of it matters. You center me and give me balance. You are the light to my darkness. The sweet to my bitter. We belong together. You are a shoulder to lean on when times are hard and the best friend a person could have. I love laughing with you, drinking with you, working beside you, and just being in the same room as you. I'm privileged to know you and pity anyone who misses the opportunity to do so. I don't want to live a day of my life without you." I lean up and graze his forehead with my lips, kissing him tenderly and gently, his eyes remain focused on me. "So. You can run away from this, from me, and leave it all behind or you can stay...and marry me."

Chapter Seventeen

Brandon

Every argument I had been making in my head fades from my mind at hearing those two words and my mouth hangs open at the shock of it. This conversation has taken a full course turn and has headed down quite an unexpected road and I'm at a loss for words. Marry him? Did I hear him right? I know I did. My tears have been free flowing for some time and his question just encourages more to fall.

His lips are on my forehead again and I want to stop him being so close, but I can't. His touches feel so good, so right, and they are steadily tearing down my defenses.

"Don't think about it, Brandon. Just say you will." He removes his lips and replaces them with his forehead, bringing himself closer as he gazes into my eyes.

"I've been stripped of who I am. How can you want me?" I ask.

My heart pounds in my chest, harder with each passing instant. All I want to do is fall into his arms and be wrapped up in his embrace and pray for everything horrible to be wiped clean from my mind, but I can't. How unfair to allow myself to go back to that life.

"How can I not want to be with you? I hate what's been done to you and how badly you're hurting because of it, but the only thing that matters is that you are by my side always. I swear to you, Brandon, no one will ever use you in that way again. Maker help me, you will know nothing but a loving touch from this day forward. I promise you. Say yes, babe. Marry me. Spend the rest of your life by my side and know that you are loved beyond words."

Alistair brings his hands down from my face and takes ahold of both of mine. The fight drains from my body and I make feeble, pointless arguments trying fruitlessly to dissuade him, knowing I cannot possibly be desirable any more.

"We can't. There is no way it will be allowable. You know this."

"Says who. I'm in charge, there is no law stopping us and I'll marry whomever I damn well please to marry, and I want that person to be you, Brandon. Say yes."

"What of an heir? The council has pushed the issue for years, what of that? We've looked down this road before, Alistair, and you know it's one we can't take. They won't back down on this issue, you know that."

"Either way, it was going to be a problem for me. We'll sort it out, one way or another. I can't be the only King in history not to have children. Now, are you just going to keep looking for reasons to avoid the question or are you going to answer me."

"Even after everything you know, you still want me? Alistair-"

"I want you more than I want my next breath, more than life. Marry me, Brandon."

I draw my bottom lip in my teeth and meet his eyes dead on. Barrier? What barrier? Yeah, there it goes. Shattered into a million pieces. My heart swells and aches for this man before me. All I can do is nod. Words escape me and my stupid tears won't stop falling. The instant I acknowledge his question, Alistair's mouth captures mine and he kisses me.

It's been a long time since I felt his lips together with mine and their warmth and taste have me falling into his arms. My lips fall from his and I collapse against his chest gripping him with all the strength I have left. I bury my face into the crook of his neck and let everything from my past drain from my body into him, needing him more than I thought possible. Alistair just holds me; cradles me in his arms and doesn't let go.

"We'll get through this, B. I'll never let you go. I got you, babe."

Maker how I love hearing him call me that. I don't know where it came from, but I don't want it to stop.

* * *

I don't remember falling asleep, but when I wake up the sun is reflecting brightly in the room and the air in the cottage is cold. Alistair's warm body is wrapped around me, holding me tight to his chest and the blankets are pulled up to my chin.

I struggle to open my eyes more than slits. They are puffy from a night of crying, they sting and feel raw. Alistair stirs under me and brings a hand to stroke my hair.

"Are you awake?" He asks.

"Yeah."

I raise my head to meet his eyes and rest my chin on his chest. He studies me and brings his hand to trail down my face to my lips. The concern in his gaze makes me wonder just how awful I must look.

"Do I need to worry about you fighting me off any longer?"

Frowning I shake my head. "No. I'll… In time, I'll be okay."

"I know you will. I believe in you, Brandon."

We lay in silence for a long while. With a gentle touch he traces the lines of my face as he hides behind a look of concern and longing. It is only now that I am able to see how much of a toll this journey has taken on him as well.

"What are you thinking?" I ask.

Alistair gives me a tentative smile. "About that kiss last night. I've missed kissing you." He draws his thumb over my bottom lip. "Brandon. Is there any chance you-"

I don't let him finish and raise myself up to collide my lips with his. I'm not sure why I do it except the feeling of deprivation that has taken hold in my body is telling me it's okay and I should.

I haven't allowed myself to think of Alistair for so long that when I opened my heart back up to the idea of him again last night, it was like a flood of need and desire pouring through my body; one I had been suppressing and thought I could go without. I need this kiss, and him, more than the oxygen in my lungs; more than the pain that has settled in my heart. He was the only thing that was ever right in my life and I was ready to throw it all away.

As the darkness inside me lifts, Alistair teases his tongue with mine and I don't hesitate to give him more of what he seeks. He takes my hips and pulls me up closer to him, diving his tongue into my mouth further still. I delve deeper, lapping up the sweet taste I've missed so much, crushing our mouths and bodies together. All the confusion in my mind is evaporating and all that is left behind is the longing need I've always had for this man.

I didn't think I could ever come back to this place again. I was certain all hope for a life with Alistair was gone, but as I feel his familiar taste dancing across my palate and the warmth of his body nestled against me, I realize he's all I want in the entire world and maybe I can forget the past again. Maybe.

We kiss passionately for a long time, hardly able to get enough of each other, trying to make up for lost time. It's desperate and frenzied, laced with a fear of something we almost lost. The pull toward Alistair is so strong, all I can do is just go with it.

Only when I feel Alistair's arousal pressing hard into my thigh does our kiss stutter. I'm ripped back into the present as an unexpected rush of anxiety prickles across my skin. I skitter up and away from Alistair so fast I nearly fall off the other side of the bed as terror fills me up. The dirty feeling of having been used washes back over me and I'm reminded why I was trying to leave in the first place. Stunned that Alistair somehow made me forget.

He picks up on my panic instantly and snags my hand as he scrambles after me, keeping me close, probably fearing I will run away.

"We can stop. Brandon. Look at me. It's okay."

My wide eyed gaze drifts to another place as I fight off memories of the past. Images of Rovell and the trapped, suffocating sensation of being stuck underneath him as he used me for his own sadistic purposes. Flashes of a frightened child, crying in the corner of his room. The sickening weight of being at another person's mercy and not having a fighting chance. These thoughts and more all dart into my mind without warning and I can feel my heart racing out of control inside my chest.

Alistair manages to pull me back to the present with his gentle coaxing and I refocus on the dazzling blue of his eyes in front of me. Alistair. My Alistair. The man who has been my rock without my even knowing it. He grounds me back to the here and now as I study him and the concern playing wearily across his face.

"Are you sure you want me, Alistair? I'm really messed up. So much has happened to me. I'll understand if you change your mind. I've been-"

"I want you, B. Believe me. Nothing you've told me will change the way I feel. I know this can't be easy for you. We don't have to do anything right now. Not until you are ready. That was too fast, I'm sorry. Ignore my damn cock, it has a mind of its own. I've just missed you so much. I missed your lips, and you being in my arms. It felt so amazing just to hold you last night."

It had. It was the best night sleep I've had in a long time. My nightmares, for once, had gone and waking up in Alistair's familiar embrace had set my mind at ease for the first time.

Fear still sits like a lead weight in my gut. A combination of memories, new and old, keep pummeling at my brain. With the uncertainty over how I will recover and bury my past again rolling around my head, I just sit and stare into Alistair's eyes. It all makes my heart hammer a little harder and causes an unstoppable tremble, like a shiver that I can't shake off, to radiate over my body. I can't understand how Alistair can look past everything I have told him and still want me. How can this be okay with him?

I look down to where Alistair has begun caressing my hands. It feels good and the urge I once had to pull away has diminished to something more controllable. I hate to admit how badly I need him right now and how badly I want him to make love to me. I want to tell him how the flashbacks of what Rovell did are burned inside my mind and I want him to throw water over those thoughts and douse their flames. Replace them with good so I won't feel their agony every time I close my eyes. Erase it from my body and create a new picture in its place. One of renewed love and joy that I'd feared I'd lost. I hate knowing Rovell was the last person to have me and I want that amended.

My body feels violated and dirty. I want to scrub all the shame away and be clean again. I want to be free of the ugliness I feel inside, the taint Rovell's touch has left behind. I need Alistair. I need him to help me forget. Paint me a new picture. Give me renewed hope. Maybe then I can feel whole again.

Without words, unsure I can explain my needs in a way he would understand, I lift my chin to meet his eyes, lean in and kiss him instead. It is tentative at first because when I close my eyes all I see is Rovell, but I take that vision and push it away. I fill my thoughts with Alistair, as best I can, and use his familiar taste to keep me grounded in the here and now.

Alistair is hesitant against me and slow to move forward. He hasn't stopped me, but I know it will be up to me to take this further if that is where I want to go.

With encouragement, the heat in the kiss rises and before long it turns hungry. I'm doing everything to be closer to him.

Forcing my mind to remember this man and all the good that goes with him. Even with the growing intensity I'm showing, I can feel Alistair holding back. I pull away again, panting against his mouth, exhaustion from having had little to eat making me light headed as I gaze into his eyes.

"I'm okay, Alistair. I want this. Please. I need it."

"Brandon. I'm worried about you."

"Please. I need you to make it good again. I need to forget."

I dance kisses up his neck to his ear, drawing his soft lobe into my mouth, teasing it with my tongue, suckling gently, just how I know he likes it. He can't hide the moan when it escapes his lips and it brings the first smile I have smiled in ages to my face.

My horrors stay just out of reach in my mind; hovering close where if I tune into them, even a little, they threaten to cripple me. I draw up the rest of the strength I have and keep them at bay. I forgot how much I love bringing this man pleasure and I use it as my driving force. Enticing more noises, I grind my stiffening cock to his, elated when he gasps and grips my waist tighter, digging his finger into my skin.

"Make love to me, Alistair." I whisper in his ear.

He pulls his head back from my attacks and turns to look at me, breaking my mouth free from his earlobe.

"Brandon. It's too soon."

"No. I need this. Make me forget. Please."

Alistair watches me as he brushes a finger over my lips. "Are you sure, babe? I don't want to push you. I know with everything…"

"Unless you don't want me anymore…I need to feel you inside me, Alistair. Please."

"Maker help me, B. I want to. I desire you. I missed being with you. I don't want you doing this for the-"

"Then take me. Don't make me beg."

He hesitates a moment more before crashing his lips into mine again and this time I can feel him let go of his worry as he presses me to continue.

I need this more than I realized. Rovell has paralyzed me into fearing my future and I need to take his power away. I don't want to live under his control anymore. I want to break free. I want to take back the life I made. It can't be too late.

Being here at this moment in Alistair's arms, kissing him, is like coming home. He is the one constant in my life. The one thing I've always been sure of and the one thing I was terrified I needed to let go of. I was wrong. For whatever reason, Alistair never pushed me away, or showed any disgust in knowing all the dark secrets there were to know about me. Instead he embraced me whole heartedly. He loves me in spite of my damaged soul. With him by my side, maybe I can heal.

Alistair moves his hands under my shirt and struggles to remove it. I raise my body up to help him without breaking our kiss, only parting for a moment to get it over my head and then we lock together again.

In a year and a half I have never tired of his touches. I only ever crave them more when I go too long without and right now it feels like it's been an eternity. His hands caress up my side and move to my back as he plays his finger skillfully over every fold of my muscles.

It's Alistair, not Rovell. Alistair.

The chill in the room hits my heated skin and brings goosebumps to the surface. Pulling Alistair up to sit, I straddle his lap and yank his shirt from his body. His skin is warm to touch, not clammy and smooth - *not Rovell* - it is the rough skin of a soldier and I wrap my arms around him, reveling in its feel against my own. His hands fist around my hair and hold my head in place while he delves deeper in my mouth, claiming me. The smell and taste of him is comforting and familiar. *Make me forget him. Please.*

Pulling my head back, I stare at his kiss swollen lips while catching my breath. Lush, pink, and full, not thin and almost white. I know these lips. These lips are okay.

He looks to me a little tentatively as though he sees the hesitation inside me and I try to firm my features, but I know by the slight downward turn of his mouth that I'm failing.

"Are you all right?"

All I can do is nod. I don't want him to stop. I want to erase the evil that is rotting my insides and only Alistair's touch can do this for me. I need him. *Please don't stop.*

"How do you want to do this, B? I want you to be comfortable… If you want, you can… you know."

I smile a genuine, warm smile at him. His offer means the world to me, but it's not what I want. Being inside Alistair is a pleasure that only happens on rare occasions. Ordinarily, he is more comfortable the other way around, but today I can see the concern in his face at doing anything that might cause me to be on edge. The gesture is sweet and the smile tugging at my face just goes to show what this man can do to me.

"I want you inside me. Make love to me, please. I need you."

"I'm yours, babe. If you're sure."

"I'm sure."

Rolling me to lay on my back, Alistair reclaims my mouth then continues to peck kisses along my neck, and chest as he works at removing our breeches. His eyes never stray far from my face and I know he watches carefully to ensure every move is accepted.

It is justifiable, I know I'm trembling behind my strong resolve to want this and a sliver of fear stays just out of reach, waiting to squeeze me in its grasp, one whose origin might take longer to forget then I'd like.

I close my eyes and focus on the feeling of Alistair's hands as they trail down my thighs, caressing over my skin. It's Alistair touching me and it's okay. Alistair makes me feel safe and the niggling anxiety fades away for now. I try to live in the moment and revel in the touch of my lover.

"You have the most incredible body." He breathes against my mouth. His hand trails over every inch of me, coming to rest, tentatively at first, over my achingly hard cock. He watches my reaction before he starts working me in his hand.

His lips never stop their scattering of kisses while he speaks reassurances, moving across my shoulder blades, taking a gentle bite now and then. He likes to mark me, claims he's marking his territory, but tonight he keeps his nibbling gentle and leaves my skin unblemished.

"You're mine, Brandon. Every piece of you. Never again will anyone know this body but me. Do you hear me?"

"Yes."

"Then say it."

"I'm yours."

When his blanketing kisses stop without warning, and his hand stills and then moves off me, I open my eyes to see his beautiful blue gaze looking down at me. He has perched himself on his elbow and is looking at me as though he has something to say.

"Why did you stop?"

"I know why you're are doing this, babe. I want you to know he'll never get his hands on you again and if this is what you need to erase the memory, I'm here for you. Promise you'll stop me if it's too much."

"I will."

"I need to know something else. You were upset last night. I need to know that you meant it. I want to spend every day of the rest of our lives showing you how much I love you. Say you will marry me, Brandon. Tell me again. I need to hear it."

I bring my hands to cup his face, although he shaved his beard off when we returned to the city days ago, he hasn't touched it again since and the rough regrowth under my fingers feels good and familiar.

"Of course I'll marry you, Alistair. You are my other half. I love you so much." I let my fingers trail down his back and take a firm hold of his ass in both my hands before nipping at his bottom lip. "Now claim what's yours before I have to beg."

A gentle laugh rolls off of him as he brings his mouth back to mine. Taking his time, he owns my mouth and slowly envelopes me with his love before owning the rest of my body as well.

Every touch is unrushed, every move purposeful and right. With our bodies locked together, moving in a perfect, synchronized rhythm, Alistair does just what I ask and claims every piece and part of me, washing away all the remnants of evil Rovell left behind.

I realize in this moment that it would never have mattered how far or fast I ran away, my heart would have been left behind with this man and I would never have been complete without him.

Chapter Eighteen

Alistair

I have never felt more content than I do at this very moment. The sun has fallen past midday and Brandon and I haven't left the cottage. His naked body is spooned in front of me, pressed as close as he can get and he has fallen back to sleep after a morning of some of the most intense love making we've probably ever had. Deep down, I question his reasoning for wanting to be together so desperately and so soon, but if it's what he needs to help him heal, I can't deny him.

Having him like this, wrapped in my arms, is one of the comforts I have missed over the long winter and one I feared I would never have again. I will hold him in my arms for an eternity now and make sure he always knows he is safe and accepted beside me.

I brush soft kisses across the base of his neck and nuzzle my face against him, inhaling his intoxicating scent. The temptation to stay like this the rest of the day is strong, but while Brandon has slept, my mind has been racing with all the things that need done. First and foremost; this man needs food.

The castle is probably turning itself upside down at our absence. Knowing Brandon's unstable condition, and my equally delicate one, has no doubt left everyone going out of their minds wondering what has happened to us.

Bringing Brandon home to the castle will require me to ask people to step back. He needs space and I understand his need for it now more than ever. The protectiveness I feel toward him has only increased and I will do everything in my power to help him cope with what he is going through. The sheer memory of it makes me shudder.

Who would do such a thing to a child?

Brandon is extremely malnourished and I recall Chase's constant warnings that he needs to eat because he is wasting away. I can't let him sleep all day. I need to encourage him to take some food and more than a few mouthfuls, so he can regain his strength. I feel confident he will not fight it off any longer and in a few days, he should feel less weak.

I need to talk to Eric. I don't know where the idea came from last night, but as I spilled my heart to Brandon, telling him what he meant to me, nothing felt more right than to ask him to marry me. There isn't a doubt in my mind that I want to spend the rest of my life beside this man.

I pull him snug against me and smile into his shoulder. He said yes and hearing those words made me the happiest man alive. We'd tossed the idea around before, after the trial, when the people of the city were bent on the idea that we should be wed, but we both decided it was too soon. The hundred and one ways the council may try to stop us only convinced us to give up and not push our luck. Now, today, I will not allow anything to stand in our way. I don't care how hard I have to fight for this, I will marry Brandon which is why I need to speak with Eric. I know the obstacles we will have to face and I need to find ways around them.

First being, Brandon is a commoner, and King's do not marry commoners. I don't think this will be a huge stumbling block, but it is the main reason my father and mother never married, so maybe it's a bigger deal than I understand.

Second, like Brandon mentioned, there is the matter of an heir. Obviously this is a huge bump in the road, one that may not be so easily overlooked. Regardless, I'm not going to let it get my spirits down. Brandon agreed to marry me. I'm going to revel in that joy for a little while longer before I worry too much about what could stop it from happening.

Brandon snuggles in closer to me and sighs, hugging his arms around mine, lacing our fingers together.

"You know I can hear you thinking from over here." He says, sleep heavy in his voice.

I chuckle into the nape of his neck and kiss across his shoulder.

"Sorry, but you know we should get back to the castle. I'd really like you to eat something before your body shuts down. I'd hate to think I finally got you back only to have you starve yourself to death."

Brandon turns in my arms and kisses me lightly, pecking his way across my jaw.

"A little while longer. Please. I don't want to leave your arms."

I sigh into his mouth as he returns his lips to mine and I fight the urge to give in and stay like this the rest of the day. Unable to deny his neediness, I let our tongues dance together and lose myself in a few more tantalizing kisses before forcing myself back again.

"I'm worried about you, B. You've barely eaten since we crossed back into Edovia. I'll make you a deal. We go back to the castle now, you eat a proper meal, or as much as your stomach can take while I go talk to Eric. Then, we crawl back into bed and you can have me the rest of the day and all night."

"However I want you?" I see a flicker of desperation in his eyes and it pinches my heart to see my Brandon this distressed.

"However you want me, babe."

He smiles at me and reclaims my mouth for another heated kiss.

"Why do you need to see Eric?" His lips barely part from mine.

"Because, I plan to marry you and I want all obstacles out of the way so we can make this happen as soon as possible."

"I like the sound of that."

"Me too." I deepen the kiss even more and Brandon melts into my arms

I realize it is going to be harder than I thought getting out of bed. Everything about Brandon, from his mouth to his body and soul are addicting and I can't tear myself away.

* * *

The castle is quieter than I anticipated when we enter through the doors from the courtyard. It isn't until we are on the second floor and turn down the hallway leading to our bed chambers that a crowd of people turn to us and stare, mouths gaping like we are a pair of ghosts who have just materialized out of thin air.

Chase bursts out of the clamor people and runs forward, taking in our joined hands and a smile comes to his face before his gaze rests on Brandon.

"You don't know how good it is to see you."

I notice Brandon withdraw slightly beside me. He only manages a trace of a smile before he stares at the ground and fidgets. I squeeze his hand a little tighter, giving him what comfort I can.

"Can you have some food sent up, Chase? Enough for the both of us."

Chase nods and gives my upper arm a gentle pat before heading past us down the hall.

Pulling Brandon along, we approach the gathered crowd outside our room. Eric and Fergus dismiss the four waiting guards and two maid servants with a word and once we reach the doors the crowd has been reduced to just the two men.

Fergus looks between Brandon and me, unsure what to say. The apprehension in his face is clear and I know some kind of an explanation will be needed. Fergus is one of mine and Brandon's best friends, but the nature of what Brandon reveled to me will require some amount of evasiveness when I explain things until either Brandon chooses to share his story on his own or it gets dropped all together. I will not betray his trust.

We stand in silence for a moment more before Brandon tugs my arm, bringing me closer and places a soft kiss on my cheek.

"I'm going to lie down and wait for food. Come join me when you're done."

I nod and squeeze his hand again before letting him go. When the door closes behind him, Eric and Fergus both quirk their eyebrows at me simultaneously.

"He ran last night, but he didn't get far." I stare at the closed door to my bed chambers. "I think, given some time, he'll be okay."

"He's talking." Fergus asks, only it's more of a statement than a question.

I nod. "Yeah. He broke down last night. We're… It's a long story." Remembering it all is painful and the worry I have for Brandon's recovery is real.

"Did he tell you what happened?" Fergus grabs my arm drawing my attention back to him and away from my thoughts.

"He did…and then some. I should probably make sure he's okay." Turning to leave, Eric rests a hand on the door before I can open it.

"I know you have a lot going on right now, but the people will need some kind of an explanation, Alistair. If Brandon won our freedom, however it was won, they need answers. Your own soldiers need answers."

"I can't give them answers, Eric. It's not my place."

"They don't need to know the truth of it. Just give them something they can live with, something plausible enough to get them by. You'll need to make an address."

"I will. Give me some time."

Eric nods and squeezes my shoulder before making his way down the hall. Fergus watches me and I don't immediately leave. Fergus guessed the truth while we were on the road. My facial expressions are never masked from him and I'm certain he can see the truth - or some of it - right now.

"He's going to be okay?" He asks again.

"I hope so." My voice carries more conviction than I feel.

Before I can say more, I'm being smothered by Fergus' arms as he wraps them around me and hugs me tight. The man has become far more affectionate over the winter than in the eight years I've known him. "Thank the Maker."

I hope I'm right. I hope Brandon will get through this. I meant what I said to Rovell. Brandon is a strong person and if anyone can get past this, he will. We both will.

As I hug Fergus back, a release of tension flows from my body. All the fears and worries I've been holding on to let go and I have to fight back tears that flood to my eyes, catching me off guard. I guess I hadn't realized just how much Brandon's withdrawal had affected other people. I was so caught up in myself and how I was feeling, I was oblivious. Fergus and Brandon *are* good friends and I can feel Fergus' relief in his fierce embrace.

I let Fergus go with a pat on the back. "Once I get some food in that man, I'd like to have a word with Eric. Can you let him know I'll be looking for him in a bit?"

"Of course." Fergus seems hesitant to leave. "Keep me posted?"

"I will. He'll be okay, Fergus. If I believe it, you have to as well."

Fergus forces a smile to his face. "I believe it. Take care of him."

* * *

Later in the evening, with a full belly, and the satisfying knowledge that Brandon isn't going to starve to death, seeing as he ate a decent meal with me, I send a maid servant to locate Eric and have him sent to my solar.

Sipping at a glass of whiskey, I loose myself in thought as I wait. Between Brandon and everything revolving around his return; his past, the present, and our future, I'm feeling a little overwhelmed. Brandon is still not okay, I can sense it.

Somewhere in my brain I know I also need to find time to make addresses to the people and my soldiers. Although, what I'm going to say to them, I have no idea.

Eric arrives sometime later and catches me staring into space with a puzzled look on my face.

"That is the face of a man who is thinking too hard." Eric says pulling me from my head.

I give him a smile and wave him in. As I pour him a drink, he pulls a seat up across from me and sits, crossing his right ankle over his knee. I slide him the drink and lean back letting my gaze move around the room some more.

My solar is my sanctuary. The one place outside my bed chambers that is just for me. It is also a shrine to my father. He adored art and the evidence of this love is displayed in the multitudes of paintings that can be found all around the castle. His most favorite pieces hang in this very room. I've spend many a days lost in the six paintings that hang on these walls, wondering about my father and wishing I knew the man even a little bit.

"Alistair, you wanted to talk about something?"

My father was a formidable soldier I'm told, with an eye for beauty and a soft edge. It's been said he would stand endlessly and stare at certain works of art on his wall, unmoving. A maid servant once told me they seemed to take him someplace far away, a place of contentment yet one that also brought on sadness. A place where once he was enraptured, he couldn't escape. However, she also claimed the art on these very walls were the only things that brought him peace in the end and I never understood why.

"You and my father were close, Eric. Right?"

A soft, sad chuckle comes from the man across from me. "Like you and Fergus. I was the only man who could call him out on his horseshit without offending him. I was more than his number one. I was his best friend and confidant."

"Do you miss him?"

"Everyday."

I stand from my seat and approach the painting nearest me to stare into its depths. It is a simple landscape depicting a winter forest with snow weighing down the branches of the trees. A frozen pond glistens in the sunlight while a doe and her fawn stand by its edge, ears perked as though they have just sensed evidence of danger. The soft brush strokes give the painting a gentleness and warmth, helping to convey the tranquility in the atmosphere. It is almost magical and the more I look at it the more beauty I see.

"Why these ones?" I ask.

Eric is silent for a while behind me, before I hear him shuffle in his seat and put his drink down.

"I'm not sure I'm following, son."

"These paintings, these six paintings among all the others were chosen to hang in this room, his favorite room, the one place he came to escape. Geraldine, from the kitchens tells me he would stare at them for whole days sometimes and become lost in himself. So, why these ones. Why did he choose these six specifically for this room from all the others he could have picked from?"

Again, Eric is silent. I peer at him over my shoulder and see him studying his hands.

"Do you know, Eric?"

He looks up at me, meeting my eyes. The sadness in his face wrinkles his features even more and his eyes glisten slightly as he nods his head. He doesn't speak right away and seems to be composing himself before he can go on.

"Your mother chose these paintings. On one of his trips to Dwarth, a traveling artist came through town and your mother fell in love with his work. It tickled your father seeing the joy in her face. Before we returned to Ludairium he sent us to buy all the man's finished pieces and have them sent back here. He wanted to present them to your mother as a wedding gift."

My eyes widen as I stare back at Eric. "But I thought he couldn't marry her because she was a commoner."

Eric smiles at me and tilts his head to the side sympathetically. "Your father wasn't going to let that stop him. You inherited his fierce determination, Alistair. Only, it all fell apart before he got that far."

I return to my seat and my glass of whiskey while Eric continues.

"It was right after that trip to Dwarth that the current wars over the thrown erupted into chaos and we were tossed into heavy battle. When things finally smoothed out, half a year had passed and laws were being written that kept your father put in Ludairium."

I knew those laws, they were the same laws I fought to have lifted just last winter when I needed to travel the realm and unite my armies. Laws that kept a King from venturing from his city.

"Your father sent me and a few men to Dwarth to carry word to your mother. She was supposed to return with us. While we were gone he planned to find a way to have the courts accept him marrying a commoner because he intended to ask for her hand. Well, when we arrived in Dwarth and found your mother, she was pregnant and right livid with Chrystiaan for having left her so long. Women don't understand the severity of war sometimes and pregnant ones even less."

Eric chuckles softly. "Perhaps you got your ferocity from her on second thought."

Eric adjusts himself in his seat and continues. "Anyhow, seeing Chrystiaan hadn't come to fetch her himself made her even more upset. Long story short, things got rough between them. They were two forces to be reckoned with. He couldn't go see her and she wouldn't travel to him, not in her condition. She took it to mean Chrystiaan had abandoned her and said as much. She claimed he didn't want her anymore. When in truth, he was fighting tooth and nail to find any possible way to be with her for good. It all fell apart and in the end, he didn't want to cause her more heartache so he let her move on with her life. He felt it's what she wanted."

As Eric speaks, all I can do is stare at him, drink forgotten in my hand.

"He hung these paintings here to remind himself of the woman he loved and lost and the son he never knew. You." Eric finishes.

Tears sting my eyes at his revelation and I blink a few times to clear them. Looking back to the paintings, I realize they are as much a representation of my mother as they are my father and I feel a surreal sense of peace knowing that my parents surround me in some strange way.

"But that's not why you asked me here I'm sure. Son, what's on your mind?"

I shift my gaze back to Eric and clear my throat, setting my drink down. Son. He'd been calling me that since the day I was brought here. I just hope he can understand my need with the heart of a father.

"How far did my father get with the law? Could he have proposed marriage if things hadn't fallen apart?"

Eric smiles. "He cleared it in the end, but too little too late. When he finally sorted out the law to have it rewritten, it was more than a year past. Your mother had moved on and he gave up the fight, believing she had found happiness without him. He didn't want to interfere and cause her continued heartache. He stopped the process and it was never put through."

"Huh!" I say mulling that over in my head.

"Again, what's on your mind, Alistair? I feel we are beating around a very large bush here."

I nod and pick up my glass, draining its contents before meeting Eric's eyes.

"I want to marry Brandon."

There, I said it. It's out. It's on the table. Honestly, it can't be that big of a surprise, at least to Eric. He knows the love I have for the man and has supported me since…well, since day two maybe - day one was kind of a nightmare.

Eric's eyebrow raises and he shuffles again in his seat.

"That's quite the request." He finally says.

"Not a request actually. More of a statement of fact. I'm marrying Brandon. This *will* happen. I just need to know how to get past all the horseshit barriers that are currently in our way."

Eric blows out a long breath and sits forward in his seat, drinking deep from his glass, draining it before reaching for the bottle to fill it again.

"Well from what you just told me, Eric, my father did away with the law that states I can't marry a commoner, or at least he mostly did. I can finish where he left off. That doesn't sound like a problem. In fact, if I go to see the-"

"You need and heir, Alistair, and I'm not quite sure how you see getting past this one." Eric interrupts.

"I don't want kids, Eric. No matter who I marry, I just don't. I can't be the first King to not produce an heir."

"Alistair, wanting children or not doesn't play in your decision. As King it is part of your responsibility. It's your job, probably your most important job."

"And if it doesn't happen? Then what?"

"I don't know."

"My father wasn't forced to marry and have a legitimate heir."

"No, because we all knew of your existence. We knew if he never ventured down that path, we had you to fall back on. Even Chrystiaan knew this. It was why he never pursued any other woman after your mother. He knew he wanted to give this all over to you one day. It was the only thing he could give you, since he couldn't be a part of your life."

"Eric, I want to marry Brandon. There has to be a way around this."

"There is."

I freeze with my drink halfway to my mouth and just gape at him.

"What? There is? How?"

"Give. The people. An heir."

My eyebrows scrunch up in confusion.

"I don't need to tell you how to get a woman with child, do I? The entire city knows you are well versed in the act of laying with a woman." Eric says with a hint of a smile on his lips.

"What? No. But Eric, I'm not sleeping with a random woman just to have a kid. It's not happening."

"Alistair, listen. Give the people an heir. Find a woman willing to birth and raise your child. It will not be a difficult task, women swoon at your feet. I've seen them. Offer to provide for her and the child, the crown can do that you know, and then you can be free to marry Brandon without any more barriers and not have the responsibility of a child if you don't want one. I don't necessarily think everyone will condone you purposefully fathering a bastard and marrying a man, but it's an answer to your problem. You can legitimize the birth just as your father did yours. The council will have nothing to fight."

I'm sure my jaw is still on the floor as I gape at Eric's nonchalant solution to my problem. Is he serious? The man's out of his tree.

"And what exactly do I say to Brandon? 'Oh sorry, B, just got to go get my cock wet with some wench at the tavern tonight…Hope she gets pregnant, if not, I'll just have to have another go.' Do you realize what you are saying to me?"

"I do. Maybe it's not ideal, but if you want to marry Brandon, that's your solution. Take it or leave it."

"Come on, Eric. What about appointing an heir? Why isn't that an option?"

"Because you aren't dead, Alistair. Do you know the Ellesmere family name has held the crown for over two hundred years? The last thing the council will allow is for you to appoint an heir and break that inheritance because you are too damn selfish to carry it forward."

"Oh yeah?" Tendrils of heat burn inside me. I slam my glass on the desk and stand to glare down at Eric. "Selfish?!? It was the bloody council who were ready to hang my ass just last winter and you're calling me selfish? Well they certainly had no problem with the idea then."

"Alistair, that was an entirely different situation."

"Horseshit, Eric. Not good enough. Find me another way."

"Alistair…"

I storm from the room, ignoring Eric, shaking with rage. How can it be this bloody difficult? I can't go through with what Eric suggested. There has to be some other way. What the hell am I supposed to say to Brandon?

I detour the halls in the castle taking the longest way possible back to my bed chambers. I need to cool off before I face Brandon. He's already in a fragile state of mind. My coming back all hot with anger will not help anything.

Chapter Nineteen

Brandon

I knew right away when Alistair returned that his talk with Eric hadn't gone well. He couldn't sit still and his poor thumb was taking abuse from his teeth like I've never seen before. All I can do is watch him. I know he is trying to find a way to put whatever it is to words because every so often during his dizzying pace of the room he stops and just looks at me. His mouth opens and closes again and again and he wrings his hands before continuing to pace.

After about two dozen trips around the room and half as many failed attempts at saying anything to me, I fly off the bed and grasp him by his upper arms, halting him before he wears out the soles of his boots, or the floor, or both.

"Just say it already. Good grief I can't take watching you walk in circles anymore."

Alistair's beautiful blue eyes are troubled and I take a finger and try to smooth the creases in his forehead before they become permanent.

"Alistair, talk to me." I urge again.

He blows out a breath and takes my hands in his.

"I'm still working it out. There's nothing to say yet."

"Horseshit! So you're saying that you're pacing a hole in the floor for no reason?"

He breaks eye contact and shuffles on his feet like he wants to get away.

"What did Eric say, Alistair?"

He goes to turn, but I spin him back around and hold him in place.

"Spit it out. What did he say?"

"I need an heir."

I knew it. Every time we've ever discussed the possibility of getting married, this was where we were halted and the subject would be dropped.

I was shocked by Alistair's proposal last night and the adamancy with which he held to it even today. He's serious this time. It's not just a passing thought or a way to keep me grounded. He quite clearly wants to do this. His determination warms my insides. I want to marry him more than anything, but we already knew what would happen if we tried to pursue it and that is exactly where we are at now. He needs an heir and I can't give him one.

The reality is, even though we have fought for a better land, with freedom of choice and openness to love whoever you choose, ultimately, we can never truly have our happily ever after because restrictions will always hold them just out of arms reach. It just feels like another reason Alistair would be better off without me. The idea had such merit too. It was freeing to think maybe we could really make it happen.

"Stop it." I lift my gaze at his harsh tone and meet Alistair's scrutinizing eyes. "You're thinking yourself out of this and I'm not giving up on us, Brandon, so stop."

"We can't be married, Alistair. It's a reality we have to accept. We already knew this. Eventually the council will come down on you and push us apart, because the bottom line is; you need an heir to the throne and I can't give you one. They all figured I was a passing fling and would be gone eventually. It explains a lot if you think about it…"

"No one is pushing us apart. I told Eric it didn't matter if I married you or a woman, I don't want to sire a child."

"And?"

Alistair slinks away from me and scrubs a hand over his face.

"And...He told me 'too bad, it's my job.'"

I stare at the floor for a long time before speaking. It always comes down to this. I shouldn't be surprised. Here I am, naïvely holding onto this idea of a perfect life I can't have and here is just another example of why it will never be. My heart aches painfully in my chest at what I'm about to say, but it's long overdue to be said and one of us needs to do it.

"Alistair...Maybe it's time we think about whether or not this relationship is going to work. I mean let's be honest here, you are the King and I'm nothing. There are details about your position that dictate your life for you and there is no way around them. I'm just in the way and I'm constantly getting you in trouble, hell I almost cost us our lives last winter. On top of it all, this shit with Rovell and my history, I'm not who you thought I was anyway. I'm not worthy of this kind of heartache. If you had any notion of the shit I'd been through, you never would have-"

Alistair's lips shut me up when they slam into mine so forcefully I'm toppled backward and stumble a few steps before landing on the ground just short of the bed. Alistair is on top of me, pinning me to the ground, crushing his mouth to mine in an angry, voracious kiss. Our teeth bang together and his tongue licks and sucks mine greedily, almost painfully.

I'm quite literally suffocating on his kiss and an unwanted panic rises inside me with the suddenness of his attack on my lips. It takes a good long moment before I can shove it down and make myself okay again.

It's not Rovell. It's Alistair. You are okay.

The fight or flight moment eventually leaves my body and instead of pushing Alistair off of me, I lace my fingers through his hair and hold him even closer. Just as I begin to feel lightheaded and on the verge of passing out from lack of oxygen, he pulls away. We both lay there, staring at each other, gasping for breath.

"I figured this might be the only way to stop those shit words from spilling off those lips of yours." He says after a moment.

I go to open my mouth and say something, but Alistair slams a hand over it and glares at me.

"Don't. Not a word about you not being good enough for me. Do you hear me?"

I nod and only then does he lift his hand from my mouth and we both just breathe and stare at each other again.

"Do you have a solution?" I ask tentatively.

"Eric had one, but I didn't like it so I told him to find me a better one. Like I said, I'm working on it."

I'm still being pinned under Alistair's weight and he doesn't seem to have any intention of moving.

"What was Eric's solution?"

Alistair shakes his head. "It doesn't matter. It's not happening. Listen, give me time, I'll sort this out and I promise you, Brandon, we will be married."

I try to find the answer he is hiding in his eyes, but he's guarded and doesn't want to let me in right now. In the past we already examined every angle of this and I already know there is no way out. I let it go…for now, but I have every intention of revisiting this again.

"Okay." I say. "Can we maybe move this to the bed? I don't know about you but I've spent enough time sleeping on the ground lately and with a bed just two feet that way," I tilt my head back, "it seems silly to lie here."

Alistair smiles and shakes his head at me.

"I'll consider moving so long as you're done trying to talk yourself out of a life with me."

I smile back at him and pull his lips back to mine, capturing them in a much gentler kiss than before. Reluctantly, letting them go, I brush another on the tip of his nose.

"I'm done." I declare. "But from this point on, Alistair, you're stuck with me, the good, the bad, the horrifying…All of it. For life. So I hope that's really what you want."

Alistair smiles back at me. His face radiates the love he has and I can see it plain.

"I'll take it all, B. I love you more than I could possibly tell you."

"I love you, Alistair."

Alistair bends his head and presses his lips to mine. His kiss is all consuming. It is far more than an ordinary kiss. He makes love to my mouth, taking me deeper into his arms. His body covers me protectively and securely as though he is sheltering me from my past, surrounding me with his own walls. I have never felt safer than I do right now.

Alistair's sensual kiss slowly becomes more aggressive when he feels me rise to him and I can feel it ringing through my entire body. Even after all the times we've been together, Alistair is able to make me feel things like I've never felt before. My body responds to his every touch and he knows it.

Tearing away from my mouth he brushes his lips down my neck. I tilt my head to the side, giving him all the access he needs and I suck in a sharp breath and gasp as his teeth clamp down on the base of my neck, marking me. His wicked mouth bites and sucks at my neck sending shivers to run up my spine while also sending my cock to twitch. Alistair chuckles as he continues his assault, clearly feeling my arousal. This time my thoughts are more grounded and my fear manageable.

"Bed." I manage to say as Alistair's greedy mouth takes another hefty bite at my shoulder making me shudder with desire.

Taking his hot mouth off me, Alistair gets to his feet and helps yank me up as well. His hands are all over me, ridding me of my clothes as he backs me toward the bed. I tear his shirt over his head and shuck his breeches a fraction of an instant before I'm falling backward again, only to land on the soft blankets this time instead.

Alistair's warm, naked body comes down on my own, covering me, wrapping me up as he reclaims my mouth. He dominates all my senses, keeping my insecurities at bay, not allowing them a chance to claim me.

The faint smell of wood smoke mixed with the pure essence of Alistair tickles my nose. A trace of whiskey that I associate so much with our daily life invades my pallet when he dips his tongue in my mouth. My skin prickles under his touch and his whispered words of desire only make my body tingle in anticipation.

When he releases my mouth again, I open my eyes and my breath is taken from me seeing the beauty of the man wrapped all around me.

Alistair. My Alistair.

Overwhelmed is the only way I can describe the flood of emotions I'm feeling. I stop for a moment and just stare at him, amazed that I have found this kind of love in my life. I feel truly blessed to be here right now. As though life has given me a second chance and for the first time, I am free from the nightmares of my past.

Alistair's face becomes concerned as I watch him.

"Are you okay?"

He asks me that so often now.

"More than okay. Just really overwhelmed with love right now. Feeling truly grateful."

Alistair traces his thumb across my cheek and swipes away a tear I didn't even know had fallen.

"I'm right there with you, babe."

When our lips come together again, our bodies aren't too far behind. Alistair makes love to me entirely. Mind, body, and soul. If ever there was a doubt left in my head about where I belonged it is all erased in that moment. I know without a shadow of a doubt that I'm Alistair's and he is mine. Nothing can stop our love, we are bound to each other and no matter the obstacles; we will fight our way through anything life throws our way.

* * *

Exhausted, yet completely sated, I curl up against Alistair's side and rest my head on his chest. He runs his fingers through my hair as I listen to his heart slowly calm under my ear.

"What did Eric suggest?" I figure now may be a good time to get this out of Alistair. He is relaxed, sleepy, and after the intensity of our love making, his stress must be completely wiped out; for the moment at least. He's always the most agreeable after sex.

"It's a terrible suggestion, B, and I have no intention of following through with it."

I wait, but he doesn't divulge any more information. He's pretty adamant about keeping this to himself.

"Okay, I get that, but what was the suggestion?"

He sighs heavily under me and wraps his arms secure around me.

"Okay, but if I say this, you need to understand that under no circumstance will I even consider this as an option. I don't want you to even worry for an instant that I will."

"Okay." I peer up at him, curiosity piqued and see I have succeeded in putting the worry right back on his face. So much for stress free. Clearly the moment has already passed.

"He tells me I should find a woman willing to have my child and raise it. Offer them financial stability for their entire lives and then I'd be free to marry you. The child would be a bastard like I was. I would then need to legitimize the birth with the courts and the people would have their heir. A child of my blood. Then I could be free to be with you."

"Oh." It's the only thing I can think of to say.

A silence falls between us before Alistair rubs a hand up and down my back.

"You caught the beginning of that where I said it is *not* an option, right?"

"Yeah." I say. "It's just harsh to hear."

"I told Eric to find an alternative. I wouldn't be the first King in history to not produce an heir. I know it breaks the bloodline, I get that, but bloody hell, they were ready to hang me last winter. They would have had to appoint an heir then. Why does it have to be such a big deal now? It shouldn't be this complicated?"

I scoot up on the bed so I can face him and try to kiss the worry out of his wrinkled brow.

"Eric will come through for us, Alistair. He always does." I'm not sure I believe my own words. We've know this truth for a long time and I'm not really sure why Alistair is so surprised at what Eric has told him. But if anyone can get him out of this, or at least convince the council that appointing an heir is acceptable, it will be Eric. And for Alistair's sake, I hope he pulls through.

Chapter Twenty

Alistair

I left the warm confines of my bed and the body of my sleeping lover to cross the city through the brisk - and I mean very brisk, more like, down right freezing - spring morning air. After an evening of mind-blowing, fully gratifying love making, one would think I would have slept better than I did, but as the first rays of morning light glistened across the sky, I laid wide awake humming with nervous energy and needing to put things right so I could fulfill the promises I made Brandon.

I snuck gracelessly out of bed, stubbing my toe in the dark and rhyming off a good smattering of curse words, waking Brandon in the process. Luckily, he mumbled an understanding when I told him I was headed out to see Fergus, rolled over, pulled the covers back over his head, and was asleep again before I made it out the door.

Making my way through the city streets, just as dawn crests the horizon, I'm in time for the city to begin coming alive. Crossing through the market, I already have to dodge around a half dozen men setting up their carts to sell their wares for the day. Other vendors have been prepared for a while and are sitting in wait of the slow building crowds of people making their way out into the streets.

I shiver in my jacket and pull my shoulders up near my ears, trying to block out the winds that are making them ache.

Fergus lives just west of the market square, a few roads up and away from the bustle. I pass eager men and woman going in the opposite direction and give them a smile and nod when I am greeted; always by name and never by title.

Bouncing on my feet at Fergus' door, more to keep my blood flowing than for any other reason, I wait patiently after having knocked twice already. I can hear the squeal of a child's voice followed by the pitter pattering of running feet followed then by a deep commanding "Benjamin George, sit back down at the table and listen to your mother before I tan your ass". I shake my head and knock for a third time; louder to ensure I will be heard. *And people somehow think this is a life I would want? Not a chance in hell.*

A piercing scream erupts from within followed by a "Daddy, nooooooo" wailing. A moment later the door before me is yanked open and a flustered Fergus stands before me, half dressed and looking completely frazzled.

"What!" Is all he can say to my smiling face staring back at him.

I shake my head and laugh. "I put you in charge of hundreds of men on the field and you can't handle one sticky-fingered toddler? I'm surprised at you, brother. What are you going to do when there are two of them running around?"

"Hang myself. What do you want? I'm going to be late, I'm supposed to be on the field training this morning."

Jordan, Fergus' exceptionally pregnant wife, appears behind him with said toddler balanced on her hip. Benjamin's long dark hair falls into his face and his eyes light up when he sees me. He glances past me and frowns.

"Where 'nuncle Nanon?"

"Uncle Brandon is sleeping still. I came to talk to your daddy, lil B, is that okay?"

He smiles and tucks his face into the crook of his mama's neck.

"Good morning, handsome." Jordan says, planting a kiss on my cheek. "Come on in. Ferg is not in as big a hurry as he makes it sound. He's just being a crank bucket. Are you hungry? I have a whole pot of porridge on."

"Thanks, beautiful. That sounds great."

"Quit hitting on my wife, ingrate." Fergus says with a shove to my shoulder.

I stick my tongue out at him and laugh. "What? She started it."

Jordan and I have always got along well and like to drive Fergus crazy with harmless flirtations whenever we are together.

"Why are you here this early? Is Brandon all right?"

"He's coming around. We're doing okay. Lot of shit came into light over the last few days, but nothing we can't work through."

Fergus takes me into the dining area and we sit at his solid oak table that could easily sit a family twice as big as Fergus'. Little Benjamin sits, bouncing on his knees in the chair across from me, chewing excessively on a heel of bread as he watches me. His little dark eyes keep checking the door and I know he's waiting for Brandon to show up. I rarely make visits to Fergus' house without Brandon and the little guy has become quite fond of my man. In truth, I think my big B is quite fond of lil B too. I smirk at his restlessness and turn my attention back to Fergus.

"I asked Brandon to marry me." I say to my long time best friend.

Fergus' eyes go wide. "Holy shit!"

"Ferguson Harris, watch your mouth in front of your son." Jordan reprimands from the kitchen.

"Are you serious?" He asks lowering his voice.

"I am. And he said yes."

"Holy shit." Fergus says again, only this time it is more of an under his breath kind of whisper and his face turns to a grin.

Jordan comes in and puts two bowls of porridge down in front of us and lifting Benjamin to her knee, steals the boy's seat beside her husband.

"What's got you all a cursin'?" She asks.

"Brandon and I are getting married." I tell her.

Jordan smacks Fergus' arm. "And this shocks you, Fergie? I told you it would happen." Turning to me she adds. "I get stuck with this shmuck and you get sweet, angel faced Brandon. Where did I go wrong? Seriously?"

I give her a warm smile. Jordan has always loved Brandon, even way back when Fergus and I were still trying to sort him out she was sucked in by his charm.

Fergus is still shaking his head at the news, mouth gaping a little.

It's nice to have the support of friends. Not that I think I won't get support throughout the city as well when we tell them, but from the people I care about; it means so much more. I have to admit, Eric's reaction kind of stung. I was hoping the man would have been more supportive, but I guess I can understand he's just looking out for me.

"Well it's not all sunshine and roses just yet," I explain, "we've hit a pretty big snag and I'm not sure how we're going to work around it."

Jordan and Fergus share a sympathetic look and I can see right away this has already been a discussion they've had.

"An heir?" Fergus asks by way of confirming his thoughts.

I nod and start stirring my porridge around in my bowl.

"What are you going to do?" Jordan asks as she bumps her knee, trying to settle the now squirming child on her lap.

I let out a heavy sigh, dropping my spoon back down without taking a bite.

"Eric is supposed to be trying to find me an alternate plan because his original one pissed me off and I refused to go through with it."

"What's that?" Fergus asks.

"He wants me to choose a woman, impregnate her, insure to keep her and the child taken care of, and legitimize the child's birth like my father did. Then, and only then, will I be free to marry Brandon. The bloody man insists I give the people an heir."

"So have you talked to Brandon about this?" Fergus asks.

"Yes. And I told him there was no way it is happening and Eric *will* find another way. He'll just need to convince the council I can appoint one."

"So you didn't even discuss with him if it was a feasible option. You decided for him."

"What!?! It's *not* a feasible option, Fergus. I wouldn't even consider doing that to him."

"I'm just saying maybe you should have asked him his thoughts. How do you know he wouldn't have been okay with it? This would mean he finally gets to marry you. It would alleviate the final huge stressor in your life. I'm just saying maybe you shouldn't have decided for both of you."

"Are you serious!?!" Fergus is making no sense. I figured I'd come here this morning for some support and let all this shit off my chest and here Fergus is agreeing with Eric. "Jordan, is he serious?"

I look between them in shock at what I'm hearing. Jordan puts a hand on Fergus' arm and looks to me with questioning eyes.

"I think what my insensitive, idiot husband is trying to say, Alistair, is this; *you* already know in your heart you have never wanted to have children. You made that clear repeatedly over the years, but have you ever asked Brandon his thoughts on the matter? Did you ever think maybe deep down inside Brandon might have a longing to be a father and here you are in a position - albeit not an ideal position - to give him a child and make your realm happy in the process? Maybe, just maybe, he wouldn't be entirely against the idea."

I feel like I have been punched in the chest and all I can do is stare blankly across the table. The thought had never crossed my mind. Brandon and I have never had any reason to ever even discuss this line of thinking because children were just deemed impossible. I have no idea if the man I love and care for so deeply has ever aspired to be a father.

As my body catches up with my mind, I slowly close my gaping mouth and shake my head. "But I can't do it. Even if Brandon wanted this, I don't think I could bring myself to being with a woman again and not feeling horrendously guilty about what I was doing. I mean, come on, what if it was you guys? Ferg, what if you and Jordan couldn't get pregnant and the only way to make it happen was to send her off to bed another man. Are you saying you could do that and be okay with it?"

"I'm saying if Jordan and I wanted it badly enough and it was the only way, and it was required for some reason, I think we might see a way to make it work. Maybe consider a close friend we felt comfortable with, who we could trust."

"Are you saying you'd let your wife sleep with me?"

"Like hell. Jordan is not having your baby, she's busy enough having mine." Fergus gives her bump a gentle rub.

"Do you see what I'm saying?"

Jordan leans forward best she can and gives my hand a gentle squeeze. "Alistair, maybe you should talk to Brandon. There are options. What about Sam? You and Sam have history, maybe it would help it feel less tainted in your mind if it was someone you knew."

"Yeah," Fergus adds, "You and my sister were involved for a while. It's not altogether a bad idea."

"Are we having this conversation? Do you two not hear yourselves? Sam and I have a history, sure, so do me and half the bloody women in Ludairium. I'm not doing this. There has to be another way."

I push back from the table having fully lost what little appetite I had. I can't understand why people can't see this from my perspective.

"Excuse me. I have to go."

I take off to the door feeling the hot anger brewing inside me again. This whole situation is ridiculous. Why is this so bloody difficult? Why is it so important that the throne stay in the bloodline? I've about had it with being the only Ellesmere left in all the realm. I wish my father had had the forethought to at least have two children in case the first one was a royal mess, which I clearly am.

I make my way back through the city toward home. The market is in full bustling, busy mode now and it slows my stride to nearly a crawl, aggravating me even more.

When I return to mine and Brandon's room, I find him curled up in a chair with a blanket wrapped around his still naked body and he is simply staring out the window with a look that is so far away. He makes no acknowledgement of my presence at all until I kneel down in front of him and take his hand in my own.

"You okay?" I ask.

He gives a weak smile and a nod. I'm not buying it. The turmoil inside him is clear. No matter how recovered he can seem when we are together, I can't forget the scars this man has deep inside. They may take a long time to heal. Any ordinary man would be crippled if they had to deal with what Brandon went through.

"How's Benji?" He asks.

I study Brandon, seeing the mixture of different emotions playing across his face. The stress of this past winter's trauma is evident, but a hint of contentment and hope appears at the mention of Benjamin's name. Brandon has always had a good bond with Fergus' son and watching that small amount of peace cancel out his anguish, even briefly, makes me wonder if Fergus and Jordan may be right.

How could I not know this about the man I love? How is it we never talked about this before? Well…I suppose…What reason would there ever have been to talk about it?

"He's giving Fergus a run for his money as always. He asked where you were."

Brandon smiles. "I haven't seen him since I left to go north. I bet he's grown."

"Yeah, a lot actually. He's going to be the spitting image of his father; poor sot."

"Does he still call me Nanon?"

I laugh softly. "Yup…That he does."

I watch a sparkle generate in Brandon's eyes as he talks about Benjamin. The first true sparkle I've seen since the vacancy left only days ago and a lump forms in the pit of my stomach as I realize I may have selfishly been making decisions without knowing how Brandon truly felt. I assumed I knew what the right answer was and I can see now, I could be wrong.

"B? I have to ask you something and I want you to be completely honest with me."

Instantly the sparkle is gone and worry sinks back in darkening the gray of his eyes. He's become so fragile I can visibly see him pull away at the slightest of things. I hate to see him like this and wish I could just take it all away; everything from the past winter and all the shit from his childhood and give this man the peace he deserves. I have to trust that time will help heal him and it will not be like this forever. Hell, if I can give this man peace. I will do it at any cost.

"B. Have you ever had the desire to have children? To be a father? Is that something you've ever wanted in life?"

He is taken aback by my question and the worry turns to confusion and he just blinks at me as though I'm supposed to say more.

"Have you?" I urge.

"Umm… It's never been an option with me. I mean, I knew it couldn't happen so I guess I never really put much thought into it… Why?"

I take Brandon's hands in mine and caress them, giving myself some balance and hoping to do the same for him. I feel suddenly nervous and I hope my voice doesn't shake when I say what needs to be said.

"Well. I want to give you something to think about. Don't answer me right now. Really think about it. All of it. Okay?"

"Okay…" He says wearily.

"Since coming to Ludairium and taking my place as King, I have been reminded, nearly daily, of my responsibility to give my people an heir. The crown has stayed in my family for hundreds of years. Ellesmere is the longest bloodline to hold the title and I'm it. The only Ellesmere left. I've kicked up a fuss about it since day one. I've never seen myself as a father and couldn't fathom how I could ever follow through with what was being asked of me. I guess I always figured maybe when I was older I would eventually crack and do what was expected, but the years keep passing by and I haven't changed my mind."

"It's not like you're that old, Alistair."

"I know, but regardless. Anyhow, then I fell in love with you. I want to marry you and spend every day of the rest of our lives loving you. Eric tells me I have to have an heir before I can be permitted to do that. Like I said to you last night, I told Eric to find me another way; that there was no way I would ever do what he suggested to our relationship. I'm telling you, Brandon, if there is no other way, if they refuse to allow me to appoint an heir, I will lay down my crown tomorrow and walk away from it all to be with you. The Ellesmere line will die with me. They'd have to appoint a King anyway. I'm okay with that. The realm will be furious, but since when have I ever done what is expected of me?"

"Alistair-"

"I'm not finished," I give his hands a squeeze and lift myself up to give him a soft peck on the forehead. "Hear me out, babe. Please. This morning, I went to see Fergus and Jordan and they said some things that made me think." I take a deep breath before going on. My mouth is dry and I realize I'm more nervous about presenting this than I thought.

"If fatherhood is something you want; it's something I can give you. If I do what Eric suggests, the people will have their heir and you and I can raise a child together. It won't be your blood, but that child will be yours and mine. You could be a father. Don't get me wrong. The decision to do this is a huge one because of what it would entail to achieve it. It's why I have been instant in saying no to Eric. But, if I can make a dream come true for you, Brandon, and this is something you want, I will do anything."

I think I have officially stunned him to silence. His eyes shift rapidly between my own, and his jaw hangs open. The frozen staring continues for a while longer before Brandon looks like he is trying to form words. His lips move like they want to speak, but nothing comes out right away. After a few more failed attempt, he manages to form rough words.

"I don't really know what to say."

"Then don't. Just think about it."

"But you have never wanted this, Alistair. I don't understand why you are asking me this."

I trail my thumb across his forehead smoothing the worried wrinkles away. "Because it was selfish of me to think this was just my decision. I've asked you to spend the rest of your life with me. Therefore, this decision should be made together and if it's something you want then I think we should talk about it at least and see if the method of how it would have to happen is something we are willing to live with. I'm not going to lie to you, B, I'm not sure I'd make a very good father. I curse too much, I drink too much, and I kind of have a wild rebellious side to me."

Brandon chuckles. "You think?"

"I'd do it for you. I'd do anything for you, babe."

Brandon lowers his head and brushes his lips to mine. I bring a hand behind his head and hold him close, kissing him tenderly. I wrap my other arm around his waist and Brandon leans into the kiss, deepening it. He slides from the chair down onto my lap and wraps both his arms around me, letting the blanket fall to the ground. Not for the first time, I'm aware of the profound effect this man has on me. Every word I said is true. I will do anything for him, no matter how terrifying those things could be.

Letting my lips go, Brandon runs his hands up and down my back and we lose ourselves in each other's eyes. I've always found the smoky, gray color of his eyes to be so unique; so soft and endearing.

As I stare into their depths, I notice something has changed in them. Something I hadn't noticed before now. For as long as I've known Brandon, these eyes have been guarded, shielding off secrets he never could tell the world, and for the first time that invisible barrier between him and life is gone. He has allowed himself freedom from his troubled soul and in his eyes, I can see a purity. I can see hope.

"You are so beautiful." I say without thinking. "I can't believe how much I love you."

His smile grows and lightens his whole face while he leans back in to kiss me. His kiss is raw and so filled with love I can feel it in every part of my body. Reluctantly pulling back, Brandon regards me with a serious look of contemplation.

"I'll kind of need to think about this, Alistair. It's a huge thing you are offering. I can't give you an answer right now."

"I understand, B. Take all the time you need."

Chapter Twenty-One

Brandon

Stunned might be a good way to describe how Alistair's words have left me. I can hardly wrap my head around the fact that only days ago I was running away from all of it, Alistair, this life, everything, because I didn't think I deserved any of it. Now, Alistair has proposed marriage and fatherhood in a matter of two days and the whole situation has left me…

Well… Stunned.

I left Alistair to tend to some long overdue business at the castle; things that had been neglected for far too long. Meanwhile, I have decided to take a walk to clear my thoughts and try to sort out what's in front of me.

The air still feels more like winter than the promised spring we've been anticipating and I hug my arms around me to keep the nip of the wind from traveling under my jacket. I'll be glad for the arrival of spring. I feel as though I have spent too many days dealing with cold in my bones and I'm ready to feel warm for once.

I've been circling around the empty courtyard since I left the castle not really knowing where to go. Rumors have circulated through the city about the situation in the north and the people know our freedom was bought at a cost. They may not know precisely what that cost was, but they know I came back pretty shaken up and I have no desire to face questioning, sympathetic looks right now and even less desire to come up with answers to the multitudes of questions I will be asked. I know Alistair is planning to make an announcement regarding our freedom and I know he will protect my secrets, but it hasn't happened yet, so the people are speculative and curious.

Deciding I need more than a steady pace in an infinite circle, I take the path off the courtyard that leads into the city. Halfway down this secluded little walkway, I veer off onto a less traveled trail leading to the royal cemetery. Nowhere better to find quiet than amongst the dead.

The history of the realm lies here. Men and women of Alistair's bloodline going back hundreds of years. Kings, Queens, Prince's, and Princess', carrying the Ellesmere lineage on through generations. A genealogy Alistair feels thrown into and not entirely apart of.

I can understand his loose connection with his family and his indifference in carrying on the family name and title, but I'm not sure I can condone turning away from it and pretending it doesn't exist.

I walk between the stones reading the names one by one - the stones that are still readable - committing each name to memory. This is Alistair's legacy, whether he likes it or not. This is what he was born for, even if he didn't know it for more than half his life.

Who am I to stand in the way, possibly skew something that has carried forth untampered for so long? Alistair can't walk away from this. I can't let him. Eric is right; he needs an heir.

I mull Alistair's words around in my mind carefully. If I'm being honest - and I've never admitted this out loud to anyone in my entire life - I've always felt a profound loss at the idea that I would never have children, at least not without marrying a woman and becoming someone I'm not.

There it is; what Alistair proposed tugs so hard at those buried, hidden heart strings it took everything in me not to cry right there in front of him when he mentioned it. He offered me something I had long ago dismissed and have been avoiding thinking about my entire adult life. He offered me fatherhood. The thought takes my breath away.

Every time I'm around little Benji - or lil B as Alistair calls him - I can't help but be reminded of the emptiness inside me, the gaping hole that I thought could never be filled. I love that little guy and I thought watching Fergus' son grow up, and staying a part of his life might help fill that void, but now I could have it all. A child of my own. But at what cost? Is it worth it?

The stabbing pain in my heart, knowing what would have to be done, makes me close my eyes. I have no right to feel this way. After what I did across the border…

I clench my fists and dig my nails into my palms. It hurts anyway. What a punch in the gut. The answer is so simple yet so complicated at the same time.

Logically, I know Alistair is mine. I know he loves me and would never do anything to jeopardize our relationship. I know this offer came straight from his heart and I'm the only reason he is even considering it at all. His concern is for me and me alone. I have no doubt if I said no to all of it, he'd walk away and never look back. The thing that would have to be done to make this happen, the act itself - I shudder involuntarily - would be strictly from necessity. I know this. I let out a deflated sigh. Can I do it? Can I allow this to happen?

Between what should be done for the realm and what I know I want in my heart, I think I have my answer. I just need to find a way to be all right with the process.

You have no right to be upset. None.

My skin crawls at the memory of Rovell's hands on me. I feel so dirty and ashamed. I know I chose to do what I thought was needed to save our realm, but I didn't expect to be here, embraced back into Alistair's arms with guilt staring me in the face every time I turned around. It's exactly how Rovell planed it out and damn if I can't shake it. I don't want that man to win or have any power over me anymore. Shivering involuntarily, I close my eyes and try to keep my thoughts focused on the present and not the past.

"Am I interrupting?"

Startled from my thoughts, I spin around to find Aaron Pryor, one of Alistair's newer recruits and Chase's lover hovering behind me looking uncertain as he shuffles on his feet, eyeing me.

"No. Not at all." In truth, his presence does make me a little uneasy. Between my current, perplexing dilemma and the knowledge that Chase has probably shared more information with Aaron than I would like him to know about our trip north, I'm unsure how to take his sudden appearance. Aaron and I aren't particularly close friends but circumstances that occurred last fall made us more than just passing acquaintances.

"Were you looking for me?" I ask when he makes no indication of why he is suddenly here.

"Oh. Nah. I was just out walking and saw you come up here. I'd heard you weren't doing so well since you got back. Thought maybe you could use some company. Training started back up this morning, but it was Fergus out there, not you. Kinda missed you bossing everyone around."

"Oh." Taking note that Aaron's arm is no longer slung from his break last fall, I quirk an eyebrow. "You're back on the field then I take it."

"Not yet. Well, not exactly. I should be, but I haven't done more than watch the men training so far."

"How come?"

Aaron wanders closer and plants himself on top of a grave marker in front of me, one of the ones whose markings are no longer readable. "My arm's really weak and I'm afraid I'll make a fool of myself now. It's tough to even lift a sword for long periods of time, let alone swing one around all morning. Afraid I might hurt myself or something."

I can't help the smile from sneaking across my face. Aaron has a tendency to accrue field injuries at a faster rate than any other man I've ever known. "Well that would just be true Aaron form now wouldn't it?"

Aaron pulls up a mock pout. "Careful, Captain. You'll bruise my ego and it's still a little raw. I already have a whole lot of hate for me right now because of this. But, I have a new goal to prove to you I'm a decent soldier. I just don't want to mess up again and I'm afraid it's going to be torture to get this arm back to what it was."

"You'll never grow stronger if you don't dive back in and take the bull by the horns, Aaron. No one will think you a fool. They'll see a brave man who's willing to come back from a setback in his life and live again. Don't throw away what you want because it takes a little hard work to get. Nothing comes easy in life. Sometimes the things we want most come with a price, but in the end it's worth it. You'll get there."

"Hmm." Aaron kicks his boot at a chunk of ice around the marker breaking it easily. "Maybe." We remain silent for a while longer. Neither of us really knowing what to say in each other's company.

Raising his gaze, Aaron meets my eyes. "So what has you so deep in thought, Captain?"

I study him a moment more before making a trek through the rows of stones. I'm not sure how much of personal life I feel like sharing with people just yet. "Just dealing with a lot of shit right now. A lot on my mind."

"Will you be back on the field soon?"

I hadn't given it much thought. Alistair only just decided to reinstate training sessions this morning. There are a lot of rumors circulating right now and I know what people speculate isn't too far from the truth. Once Alistair gives the people answers that will satisfy their curious minds and yet leave me with some element of dignity, maybe then. I would just rather not have to integrate myself amongst the people until such time.

"I'm not sure. I was hoping Alistair would clear up some of the rumors before I returned. I just don't want to have to get into it with everyone. It's…personal."

"Sure, I get it."

A blanket of silence falls over us again. Aaron watches the sky while I peer over to him as I continue pacing between the grave markers.

Aaron blows out a breath into the cool spring air. "So. Chase tells me he's worried about you and the King. Said you were dealing with obstacles that might threaten your relationship."

I crane my neck to look over to him a little stunned at his pointed injection of opinion "Aaron, I don't think that's any of your-"

"I'm not prying. Can I just say something?"

I lower my gaze to watch my feet as I continue weaving along the rows. My boots leaving prints behind me in the unmarked snow. What else did Chase share? "Go ahead."

"You and the King, I'm so inspired by you both. I know we don't know each other well and I know him even less, but what you both have achieved over the last year is more than I could have ever hoped for in a lifetime. Who would have thought people could have the freedom to choose who they loved, be it man or woman. I no longer have to live my life in fear because of what you accomplished. You two fought to be together and look at you. You are role models to an entire realm."

"Aaron we're not…"

"You are. I would never have been with Chase today if it wasn't for you. I don't know where I'd be right now. You know what life was like before. I have the utmost respect for both of you and I'd hate to see you fall away from each other. You two are strong enough to get through anything.

"I'm not going to say I know anything about what went on up north. All I know are the speculations and rumors that are running through the city. Chase has kept your confidence and has told me nothing. I can tell whatever happened for you to win our freedom back has scarred you to the core and you are letting it rule your life and eat you up inside. Your brave face is more troubled than you think. I just don't want to see you two ruin what you have over something that will quickly be history. Whatever happened across that border, is in the past now."

"Aaron I... You're right." I come back to sit on another stone across from him. "I'm out here trying to figure out our future actually. Alistair and I have decided to marry."

"Oh, wow." Aaron's eyes go wide as a smile fills his face. "That's incredible. The people will be thrilled."

"I bet they will. But there are things standing in our way yet before we can make it happen. That's what I'm out here thinking about."

"That's kind of vague."

"It's kind of personal."

"Fair enough. Is he worth it?"

"Excuse me?"

"The King. Is he worth it?"

I stare into Aaron dark eyes looking back at me. "He is, but that's not really..."

"Then what's there to think about? You know, a wise man once told me not to throw away what I wanted just because it takes a little hard work to get. Sometimes the things we want most come with a price, but in the end it's worth it."

I laugh at him as he recites my own words back at me with a look of pure seriousness in his face. "I said that to you just moments ago."

"Wise man." He smirks. "I'd heed his advice. I used to think he was a hard ass, but it turns out he's a decent guy. Does it fit your predicament?"

It did in a way. In order to have the life I wanted. Marriage to Alistair and fatherhood, it was going to take some work and it wasn't going to happen without a price. But, in the end it would be worth it. That much I know.

"It…It does."

"Good." Aaron nods as he stands from the stone. "Take care, Captain. Maybe I'll see you on the field soon."

"I'll tell you what, Aaron. I'll be there tomorrow morning. I expect you to be fighting alongside the other men."

"Damn. I was right the first time. You are a hard ass." He winks at me before turning to go. I watch him make his way down the hill until he disappears back down the road to the city.

I glance amongst the stones, listening to the serene reassurance of the dead and a sense of calm sinks into my bones. Alistair and I have overcome bigger obstacles and this one is bittersweet in the end. I know my decision. Sometimes in life you need to make sacrifices and I have made plenty. I have survived them all and I have come out a little stronger every time.

I turn back toward the path leading to the courtyard. I walk slow, letting the cold wind blow against my face while I let reality sink in. A smile creeps onto my face as I realize you never really know where life is going to take you and right now, I can hardly believe the future that has been offered to me.

* * *

It is long past sundown before I see Alistair again. He insisted on running his own group of men through drills tonight instead of having Fergus or Eric take his place. In truth I think he needed to bang some steel and let out the tension that had built up inside him over the winter.

When Alistair enters our room, I'm curled up with a book, not reading it, lost in my thoughts.

"How was training?" I ask as a way of breaking the tension that has blown into the room in his wake.

I can see Alistair's gaze shifting my way as he begins to undress. He's nervous and unsure how to approach me.

"It was all right. The men were asking about you. I told them you'd be back soon enough and they shouldn't worry. I kept it vague and I think they mostly got the idea that they should drop it. I'll plan an address to the people tomorrow."

"Okay. Thank you."

Silence grows and Alistair makes himself busy washing up and finding himself something to wear. I put my book down and watch him. I can see the rigidity in his body and I know he is thinking about our conversation earlier and wondering where I'm at with all of it. No sense sitting on it any longer.

I let out a shaky breath and rise from my seat by the window, leaving my book behind on the chair. His back is turned to me as he fiddles with the fire in the hearth, stoking it and adding some logs. When he stands, I wrap my arms around him from behind and draw him up against my body. He leans into me and I can feel the strain leave his body as he relaxes against me.

"Can we talk?" I ask.

He turns in my arms and regards me tentatively. I can see a hint of uncertainty in his eyes as he nods.

"Come here." I take his hand and lead him to our bed to sit. He gets comfortable beside me, but keeps a firm grip on my hand like he's afraid I may run, but those days are behind me.

"You have an answer already?" He asks.

"I didn't have to think about it too much. I already knew my decision when you asked me this morning. I just needed to be sure."

Turning my body to face him, I scoop up his other hand kissing both before continuing.

"Life never seems to cease throwing curves at me. When I look at everything I've been through in my life, I wonder sometimes how I haven't gone stark raving mad. You are the best thing to happen to me, Alistair. You have given me a life I could never have dreamed of having. Your love is boundless and I hope you know I have the same love for you too. We have taken on so much together and we always come through shining in the end. All these hard obstacles have only made us stronger. That's how I know we can take this next step without fear."

Alistair's eyes show a hint of understanding, like he knows where I am going with this, but is afraid to hear it. I'm pretty sure he has stopped breathing as he waits for me to finish.

"I want this. I want to raise a child with you. I want to be a father."

He is as still as a statue for so long, I feel I should be saying more, but that's it, that's all I have to say. A slight quiver begins in his lower lip at the same time as his eyes pool over. He grabs me in his arms and hugs me, griping me with such force I can't take a full breath. I return the hug and we just sit there, holding each other for a long time, saying nothing, just absorbing the moment before us.

"Are you sure? I mean absolutely sure this is what you want, B?" He says into the crook of my neck after a while.

"I'm sure."

He pulls back and cups my face in his hands, looking longingly into my eyes.

"I had no idea."

"I never thought it would ever be an option, so why would I ever express it to you."

"This is so huge… Eric's not going to know what hit him."

I laugh. "Considering the position you've taken on the matter for the last eight years, the poor man is going to think you're full of shit."

"We have a lot to talk about, B. I mean… How are we going to go about this-"

"Shh…We'll get there. We'll figure it all out. I know what all it entails. We'll sort through it."

"I'm going to need a lot of help. I told you, I don't think I'm really father material. I hope you don't regret this."

"I know I won't and besides, I think you're wrong. I think you'll make an amazing father."

Alistair's thumbs caress my cheeks and the smile on his face shines with such raw joy. Seeing it there, along with the tears brimming in his eyes, makes me wonder if maybe, deep down inside, it has just been fear holding Alistair back all these years. All that adamant denial has faded away so quickly, I'm not sure its conviction was ever truly real.

I move my mouth to his and take him into an all-consuming kiss. I let the twinge of fear niggling in the back of my mind fall away and open myself to the moment in front of me.

It is during the connection of that kiss that I know in my heart that we have won. Alistair and I have conquered what I was sure was the impossible. Rovell lost this fight and he will never know it. That man thought he had destroyed us from the inside and we have proven him wrong. Together, Alistair and I have the strength of an army and side by side, we will take on the world.

Pulling me down on top of him, Alistair's kisses become more desperate, more demanding. I invite every teasing demand and make more of my own. When he rids me of my shirt, I stare lovingly into the rich blue of his eyes.

"You've changed my life, Alistair."

"You've changed mine, babe." And he recaptures my lips.

All the years I spent lost in this world make sense to me now. I had been half a man, wandering aimlessly through life, not understanding the emptiness inside, until that day two years ago when I met Alistair. On that day, everything changed. I became whole. The missing piece that would fill the void I felt inside had been found.

<u>Epilogue</u>

Four years later

Brandon

"Tyler, open this door right now."

The panic has started to rise in Alistair's voice as he pounds a fist mercilessly on its wooden surface.

"No!" Comes the shriek of our toddler from inside the room where he has clearly managed to lock himself in. Again.

Alistair rattles the door knob, as though maybe shaking it a little harder might somehow dislodge it and allow him access inside. His forehead glistens with a sheen of sweat and I bite the inside of my cheek to prevent my laughter from breaking through.

"Come on. Please, you're going to get me in shit."

"Das a bad word, Papa."

"Consarn it! I know that, but I'm getting angry, Tyler. Open the bloody door."

I grin as I watch Alistair's anxiety rise. His thumb flies to his mouth where he chews it viciously as he thinks about what to do next.

I have been standing back watching this ordeal play out for far longer than I should without having intervened, but I'm amused at what's transpiring and no amount of guilt will persuade me to make my presence known.

Alistair jiggles the knob again then throws his hands up in frustration before kicking the door with a good hard thunk.

"Ty...Please."

He's reduced himself to begging now and I have to bite my knuckles to keep quiet. His knocking persists while I can hear giggles emerging from behind the barred door. I know from past experience, hearing that will only make the flames inside him grow. Alistair gets down on all fours and peers underneath, through the thin crack.

"Stop dancing around and open the door, Tyler. I can see you."

"No!" Yells the little mischievous voice from within.

"If I have to tell your daddy what you've done, not only are you going to be in big trouble, but so am I. Please open the door, Ty, I'm begging you."

"No! No! No!"

Alistair rises again and slaps a hand on the door while running his other through his tousled hair. He's practically vibrating and I can see his wheels turning as he sorts out what to do next.

"That's it! I'm going to scale the blasted terrace wall and come in there to get you and when I do you are going to get your ass tanned, young man. I swear to the Maker above." He lets out a deep growl and kicks the door one last time to drive his point home.

"No, Papa, No!" The happy giggles behind the door quickly turn into a whine.

"Yes! I'm coming around. You are in so much trouble, Tyler."

Alistair spins on his feet and nearly collides into me. The shock on his face makes me burst out laughing. He flips his head from the locked door and back to me, with wide eyes and cheeks flushing with embarrassment as he grasps for words.

"Troubles?" I ask, trying to hide my wide grin and failing miserably.

"No." Alistair says defensively. "I have it under control."

"So Tyler *didn't* lock himself in his room again and you're *not* about to scale the wall outside to the terrace to get him?"

"No... Well, maybe, but I've got this, B."

"Okay. I'll just leave you to it. So long as you don't need a hand or anything."

I shrug my shoulders and turn to walk away.

"Okay, wait." Alistair lets out a long drawn out sigh. "Please help me. He doesn't listen to me, B. I swear he does the exact opposite of everything I say. Please, please, please. I can't do this." Alistair whimpers and gives me the saddest most pathetic face to go along with his pleas.

I give a soft chuckle and kiss his cheek before walking to the barred door containing our three-year-old son. I knock a random pitter patter of knocks all across the door, covering nearly the entire wooden surface before calling out in a high, sing song voice.

"Oh, no! I've lost my baby boy. Where oh where could he be? Oh Ty-ler. Yoo-hoo? Where are you?"

Alistair frowns at me and scrunches up his nose.

"That's not going to work." He whispers.

I hold up a finger requesting silence and issue him a knowing smirk.

"Oh, no! He's gone. I've lost him. My baby boy is gone. What shall I do?" It is at this point that I pull out the fake tears and pretend to sob dramatically. Alistair rolls his eyes and glares at me with his hands on his hips.

From inside the room I can hear a shuffling and tinkering. After a moment, the door clicks and swings open. Out bounds my smiling, blond hair, blue eyed son, right into my arms. The spitting image of the man standing disgruntled and scorned beside me and with the rebellious, defiant attitude to match.

"Here I am, Daddy."

"Oh my goodness, I thought I'd lost you."

I squeeze him tight, plant a kiss on his cheek - which is sticky and tastes of honey - and swing him around to my hip. His hair is matted on top with what looks to be more honey and his little fingers appear to have a thick coating of it as well. He's an utter, sticky mess. Not surprising, it happens every time he is left in the care of his Papa.

"Are you giving Papa a hard time?"

"He say a bad word again, Daddy."

"You're tattling on me now?" Alistair says still scowling. "I let you have extra honey on your porridge too and that's the thanks I get."

I smile at Alistair indignation.

"What do you need to say to Papa, Tyler?"

"I sorry, Papa." Tyler mummers as he buries his head in my neck transferring the goo onto me now.

"Listen." I say to Alistair. "I was coming to find you because I ran into Sam in the market and she offered to take Ty for a couple nights. Did you think you might want some time for just us?"

The suggestion instantly wipes the scowl from Alistair's face and his eyes light up.

"That woman is a life saver."

It's not that Alistair doesn't have profound love for his son. He has an abundance, but true to Alistair form, he has insisted that we raise Tyler ourselves, without excess help from anybody and it's taking its toll on him. It's been me and Alistair, tag teaming all parental duties, with the occasional night or two off when he goes to be with his mother. Seldom will Alistair permit anyone else to watch our son.

Even though he gets frustrated at times, especially since Tyler has learned to walk all over him, has clearly inherited Alistair's derision for rules, and ardency for the word "no", he loves him fiercely.

He takes our son from my arms and tosses him over his shoulder letting him hang upside down. Tyler erupts into a fit of giggles as he holds a death grip onto Alistair's shirt.

"Come on, kiddo, you're going to mommy's tonight and I'm going to drown myself in a bottle of whiskey while you're gone."

"He needs washed before he goes, he's a mess. You can't send him to Sam's like that."

"Pfff...Little boys are meant to be dirty." He tells me. "Right, kiddo?" He tickles Tyler causing even more fits of laughter.

I give up. There are some battles that just aren't worth fighting. I lean in and kiss Alistair's smiling lips - incidentally, they also taste of honey. Like father like son.

"I love you, you crazy fool."

He reaches a hand out before I can get away and grips my chin, bringing my lips back in for more.

"Right back at ya, babe."

So I guess, when all is said and done, even though I needed to travel through thick and thin to find my way here, I did eventually find the perfect ending to my tale. I have a son who I love more than life itself. A husband who has never given up on me, who loves me for who I am. And freedom on soil I can call home. It turns out, I did find my happy ending after all.

The End

About the Author

I live in the small town of Petrolia, Ontario, Canada and I am a mother to a wonderful teenage boy (didn't think those words could be typed together...surprise) and wife to a truly supportive and understanding husband, who thankfully doesn't think I'm crazy…yet.

I have always had two profound dreams in life. To fall back hundreds of years in time and live in a simpler world not bogged down by technology, and to write novels. Since only one of these was a possibility I decided to make the other come alive on paper. I write mm romance novels that take place in fantastical, medieval type settings and love to use the challenges of the times to give my stories and characters life.

You can find me on Facebook and twitter.

Reviews are the best way to thank an author. Consider leaving a review on Amazon or Goodreads. Thank you

Made in the USA
Middletown, DE
04 August 2016